ATTACK OF THE
MANORWOOD BRIGADE
MAGNATH CHRONICLES

ATTACK OF THE
MANORWOOD BRIGADE

MAGNATH CHRONICLES

JOHNNY MAY

ART BY GORDON CLOVER

GRANVILLE ISLAND
PUBLISHING

Library and Archives Canada Cataloguing in Publication

May, Johnny, 1953–
    Attack of the Manorwood Brigade / Johnny May.

(Magnath chronicles ; Bk. 1)

ISBN 978-1-894694-99-5

    I. Title. II. Series: May, Johnny, 1953– . Magnath chronicles ; Bk. 1.

PS8626.A896A88 2011   jC813'.6   C2011-902252-4

Editor: David Stephens
Illustrator: Gordon Clover
Cover and Text Designer: Alisha Whitley
Proofreader: Neall Calvert

Printed in China on recycled paper.

Granville Island Publishing
212–1656 Duranleau St.
Vancouver BC V6H 3S4

www.granvilleislandpublishing.com

For my sons, Ryhal and Kieran.
I enjoyed every minute we read together,
even when I fell asleep.

CONTENTS

Cape Hookross

CAST OF CHARACTERS

Manorwood & The Valley of Stone

Terramboe	A mighty otter from Manorwood; father of Smidge.
Gerr	Brother of Terramboe.
Smidge	A young otter; son of Terramboe.
Silk (Silkena)	Wife of Terramboe and mother of Smidge.
Pete	A plump young groundhog; Smidge's best friend.
Ralph	Pete's rotund father.
Harty	Smidge's reclusive uncle; his mother's brother.
Flash	Nickname for the otter Amal, who 'flashes' a wonderful smile.
Stride	Amal's younger, fleet-footed brother.
Harnath	Leader of the Manorwood otters.
Broadtail	A young adult otter known by his unusually wide tail; steps up when times are tough.
Mash & Dash	Squirrel twins from the Valley of Stone.
Misty & Grunch	Father and mother of the squirrel twins Mash and Dash.

Magnath & The Rats	Magnath	Rat King of Magnath, ruling from Fortress Magnath.
	Jakbo	An enormous rat; once led the rat army but is now commander of the Royal Guard, King Magnath's protectors.
	Aswar	Leader of the rat army of Magnath.
	Queen Gwendolyn	Wife of King Magnath.
	Slim & Jimmy	A pair of one-eyed rat thieves wandering the Tullymug Woods.
	Bad Tooth & Knuckle Nose	Two slave-trader acquaintances of Slim & Jimmy.
Woodlanders	Marta & Alex	Sister and brother squirrels from the woodland community of Brookside.
	Duke	A reclulsive, aging rabbit living in the Tullymug Woods.
	Ting	A Woodlander mouse from Muddy Moss Moor; barter agent and leader of the Woodland Militia.
	One Eye One Shot	A squirrel with one eye who became the best archer in Muddy Moss Moor.
	Matty	A very young mouse who 'lisps' near Miss Marple.

Farlanders	Pierre & Giselle	A pair of beavers living on the edge of the Rough Wood Forest.
	Lastor the Castor	An ancient beaver, leader of the Farlanders; lives in Castorville
	Trouter (Jean la Truite)	A handsome young otter from Castorville who leads the first attack on Magnath.
Flyers	Flyboy	Leader of the flying squirrels who live in the foothills.
	General Lech	An aged flying squirrel; led the flyers in a long-ago war with the ground squirrels.
	Long Flight	A 'strong and lean flying machine' squirrel who can soar great distanes and embellish his flights with aerial stunts.
Last But Not Least	Treetop & Breezer	Two youngsters very eager to break the flyers' oath of peace.
	Miss Marple	An eccentric rat living in a ramshackle house in the foothills near Fortress Magnath who knows everything.
	Spit	A greedy mouse merchant with a dreadful sinus condition.

PROLOGUE

The biting winds of autumn came early to Magnath. For a hundred seasons, evil had resided in this impenetrable fortress of stone in the foothills of the Skull Top Mountains. On this day, as on so many others, an endless dark river flowed through a narrow pass. A river of rats. Black rats. Black soldier rats. Thousands of paws pounding out a relentless rhythm of foreboding, raising dust that was carried by the wind into the valley below.

The forests of the southern valleys were quiet, lush and green. Some of the trees on the upper slopes had turned to rich hues of yellow, orange and red like vibrant splashes of paint on an otherwise green canvas. In the fields, the hard-working and peaceful inhabitants of the valley were bringing in a bountiful harvest.

Silent and expressionless, the battle-hardened rats of the Kingdom of Magnath marched southward, eager to plunder, to loot . . . to kill.

1

ARISE AND DEFEND!

Manorwood—Southwestern tip of Cape Hookross

Many seasons ago, in the summer of the dry sun, the grain grew tall and golden and the beards on the barley heads were deep russet and as bushy as a squirrel's tail. The carrots were long and thick but sugar-sweet, and the lettuce grew waist-high. Rain came only at the absolute right time to water bountiful roots. The sun was hot, and day after day its rays cleared the clouds away to leave a deep blue sky.

The end of summer heralds the harvest, and the otters of Manorwood were energized and full of laughter as the crops were gathered. The young ones ran through the rows of green and gold, playing hide-and-seek, while the older beasts cut, pulled, stacked and carried the harvest. Later in the fall, the pups got to perform their favourite task of climbing the apple trees and throwing the fruit down for others to catch and place in wicker baskets.

News of the bountiful harvest spread far and wide. Many from the surrounding forests came to help, with high hopes of earning some grain in return. Others, such as rats and ferrets, came sneaking around at night to steal what they could carry. Patrols were organized to guard the fields and gardens at night.

The cave in the east hillside, used for storage, was quickly filling. The cool, dark, rock-walled room was protected by a large boulder, which, when rolled across the doorway, sealed in the cool air and provided camouflage. The villagers, who had never dreamed of filling the immense cavern, had no specific plan to manage the overflow, in spite of many heated discussions.

One night toward the end of harvest, Terramboe was walking along the edge of the orchard with his battle-club slung over one shoulder. The moon did not cast much light through the clouds and the darkness obscured his vision. He wasn't having any fun. Guard duty meant long hours of trying to stay awake and walking over uneven ground in the dark— tripping and stumbling over roots and stones. He couldn't use a torch to light his way; it would make his eyes useless for searching in the darkness. Ahead lay his usual resting spot atop a ledge that looked down over the village. His pace quickened at the thought of a few moments to sit and gaze at the peaceful, sleeping landscape below.

Sitting with his back against a fallen walnut tree, Terramboe opened the cloth pack tied to his waist and pulled out a pawful of dried apples and pears. They would give him energy to keep awake until dawn. Terramboe, a tall and muscular otter, normally had boundless energy, but tonight he was tired from harvesting all day.

Fighting the urge to close, his tired eyelids first widened with surprise, then squinted to make certain what he had just seen. The low bushes at the edge of the forest nearest the village and river were moving unnaturally. The tops of the bushes seemed to be undulating in and out toward the village but

2

not in unison with the wind. He couldn't make out anything else in the darkness, nor did he hear any unusual sounds, but in preparation for trouble, he dipped his shoulder, letting the strap on his battle-club slip slowly down his arm. Taking the heavy ash weapon into his huge paws, he gripped it firmly. His stare never wandered from the bushes.

Suddenly, the bushes seemed to erupt as dozens of dark figures rushed forward. There was no sound as the horde moved like a black shadow toward the village.

Terramboe leapt to his paws and ran down the rocky path as fast as his legs would allow. There was no time to organize the other guards for a coordinated counterattack, so he sounded a warning as he approached the village.

His words were spoken with such bravery and passion that they later became the famous battle cry of the otters.

"Arise and defend!" he roared as he threw himself upon the invaders, swinging his club in a vicious arc. "Arise and defend!"

The attackers were rats—in black armour and wielding spears, axes, knives and heavy swords. The smaller creatures swarmed around Terramboe, lashing at his unprotected flesh. Reacting to each new wound, Terramboe twirled to inflict death upon its perpetrator. The multitude of strikes and the ferocity of his counterattack created the impression that the mighty otter was spinning in a circle with his battle club held out like a windmill. Rats flew outward with their helmets knocked off, or smashed on so tight they would have to be buried with them stuck. Others had their chest armour collapsed so deeply by the otter's blows that they couldn't inhale another breath. The attackers started to back away, sensing the strength in their crazed opponent.

The villagers, exhausted from heavy harvest work, arose groggily from their warm beds, trying to make sense of the horrific noise outside. Hearing Terramboe's warning, most rushed to their windows to see the commotion. Those with a warrior's instincts understood there was no time to waste, grabbed the closest weapon and rushed out.

Terramboe's brother was the first to join him. Gerr confronted the black swarm, swinging his sword powerfully and with great effect. Struggling to keep up, Terramboe's young son, Smidge, dragged a stout walking stick for a weapon. When he saw a huge rat with an outstretched sword running toward his Uncle Gerr, he managed to slide the stick between its legs and trip him. The enraged attacker gathered himself up, kicked away the stick and cast an angry look upon the small otter. Frightened, Smidge ran from the raging fight.

Most villagers were slow to join the fray, and Terramboe realized the skirmish was lost. He was about to order a retreat when the clouds parted for a moment and a shaft of moonlight cast an unnaturally bright light, revealing a group of rats standing at the edge of the forest bearing a black banner with a red crest. In the centre of this group stood their leader—a menacing presence with massive shoulders covered by a flowing cape, and a head adorned by a large, ornate black helmet.

Desperate to turn the tide of the battle, Terramboe broke free and ran toward the group, screaming and pointing his club at the leader. The rat army, fearing their commander's wrath if they did not protect him, took chase, trying to bring down Terramboe with blows to the backs of his legs.

As the mighty otter's blood-stained form entered the forest, the clouds closed and the moonlight vanished. In the time it took for the villagers' eyes to adjust to the darkness, Terramboe, his pursuers and their commander had disappeared.

A few of the villagers ran toward the forest. Smidge ran until he was so exhausted, he tripped and fell. But, the chase ended when arrows, flying from the darkness, struck several of the pursuers, including the village leader, Harnath.

For a few moments, silence settled over the scene, with everyone too scared to move or talk. But soon the villagers gathered their wits and came to the aid of the wounded. Terramboe's wife, Silkena, ran to her son and calmly asked for volunteers to enter the forest to search for her husband. All the villagers who were unharmed stepped forward, but they searched in vain. Eventually, they returned to their homes.

Smidge and his mother, however, sat on a stump at the edge of the forest till morning, overcome with grief. The village had been saved by Terramboe's bravery, but this fact brought no comfort to his young son, who struggled to free himself from his mother's embrace.

"We have to try to find him," the young otter uttered, his voice thick from crying.

"I'm sure your father will be back in a little while," Silkena replied. "Besides, it is too dangerous out there for a little otter, no matter how brave."

2

THE ATTACK

Manorwood, many seasons later

The sun had finally risen high enough to warm the cool autumn air. A pattern of shadows and sunlight danced across the green forest that swept down a hillside toward the rich farmlands of the valley. By the wide, meandering river, which carved a twisted path along the valley floor, there was a clearing surrounded by tall trees. Across it, the remainder of the early morning mist lay in patches around bushes and tufts of grass.

Mixing with the mist was the steam rising off the back of a large, muscular otter. Wielding an enormous axe, his sinewy arms rose and fell in a tireless rhythm as he sliced effortlessly through logs of ash and maple. Occasionally, he stopped to toss the split wood into a growing heap, beside which a younger otter, perched on a stump, watched intently.

"You sure are strong, Uncle Gerr!" exclaimed Smidge.

"Not half as strong as your Daddy, Smidge," laughed Gerr.

Gerr and his older brother, Terramboe, had always competed to determine the most powerful one. Smidge, almost full-grown now, usually liked to hear about the rivalry between the two brothers, but this time he hung his head instead of asking for a story.

Gerr could feel Smidge's sadness and see from his nephew's slumped shoulders that he was thinking of his father, gone so long now, but still in everyone's thoughts. He stopped his work to wipe his brow and gaze at the forlorn young otter fidgeting with his slingshot. So young at the time, the poor beast's only clear memories of his father's heroics were the stories told around the village campfire. Unable to think of anything to say, Gerr attempted to brighten the mood.

"It must be about time for lunch!" he announced cheerily, adding that they must carry some of the newly split firewood back to the village. Smidge held out his arms and braced himself for the wood that Gerr would pile until the stack reached his chin. Not wanting to admit he couldn't carry such a heavy load, he staggered away down the well-trodden dirt path to Manorwood.

His uncle watched the lad weave back and forth toward the village. Wiping a tear from his eye, he put away the axe and stooped to pick up his own load of wood.

❧

When Smidge returned to the sleepy little village, his mother, Silkena, was tending to a large cooking fire that crackled beneath an oversized blackened pot. A delicious aroma of hearty food drifted through the cool air. Silkena, tall and graceful, was known as Silk, and her actions were always quick and filled with purpose.

"What are you cooking, Mom—" Smidge's voice brimmed with hopeful anticipation "—tater root soup?"

The tasty potage was an otter favourite, especially when fresh mint and clover were in season. He dropped the heavy load of split wood by the campfire and wiped himself clean of wood chips and dust.

"Well, can't you smell with that big snout of yours? Of course it is, and this is going to be a good batch, with lots to spare for dinner." Smidge eagerly ran to the walnut tree to fetch the wooden bowl his father had carved for him. As he picked up his bowl and spoon, he felt the sting of a small stone hitting his shoulder. Pretending not to notice, he reached down to pick up a napkin and quickly snatched a stone at the same time. Another stone hit him on the back. Suddenly, dropping everything, he loaded his slingshot, turned quickly and launched his stone at a dogwood bush down the hill, about five metres away.

"Ouch! You slippery, fish-breathed brute!" roared the large, slightly pudgy animal thrashing out of the bush. "Good shot, but I got you twice."

"Pete, you only got me the second time because I didn't want you to see me picking up my stone, you land-loving hog!"

They rushed toward each other with their shoulders down. Smidge tried to get as low as possible to counter the greater weight of his opponent, but Pete, at the last moment, rolled into a ball and threw himself at Smidge's foot paws.

Smidge couldn't stop in time, so his legs were swept from beneath him, and he went sailing up and over the groundhog and down the hill. Wind-milling all his limbs, he tried to regain his balance, but he landed face down in the very dogwood bush in which Pete had been hiding.

Pete lay on his back, his belly convulsing with laughter as he watched Smidge slowly slide toward the ground, the branches of the bush bending under his weight.

"Are you sure you're an otter and not a wild turkey?"

"Well, you're going to be a dead hog, not a groundhog!" replied Smidge, suspended just above the ground by one of the bigger branches.

They hadn't noticed Silk's approach, but instantly stopped their banter when they heard her voice, laden with irritation.

"Now just what are you boys doing?" she demanded from the top of the hill. "I made a good tater root soup for you, and here you are, Smidge, hanging in a bush like blown-away laundry!"

"Sorry," apologized Smidge as he untangled himself from the branches. "Hey, Mom, can Pete come for lunch?"

"I suppose so, but find Uncle Gerr and tell him that it's time to eat. I am sure he's off giving firewood away to every widow and orphan." Her voice softened with laughter.

Then she scurried off, leaving the two friends smiling, each secretly gathering a paw-full of dry leaves. The instant Silk was out of sight, they jumped to their paws and ran toward each other. Leaves went hurling up into a cloud as the two collided and wrestled each other to the ground. Pete curled into his usual defensive ball, and Smidge wrapped his arms, legs and tail around the groundhog and started tickling him.

"You're a smelly, fish-eating idddy-idddy-idddyhot!" giggled Pete. He couldn't help himself, for he was very ticklish.

Smidge found Pete's high-pitched tittering hilarious, and the two friends rolled in the leaves, laughing until tears were streaming down their faces.

જ

Lunch was a feast, the tater root soup accompanied by thick slices of bread, heavy with wildflower butter. The good food made everyone talkative, even old Uncle Harty, Silk's brother. They usually found the reclusive otter curled up with a book in his favourite place by the river. An old otter den, never finished and nearly covered with overgrown weeds and branches, served as a perfect hideout for him. Whenever there was work to be done, or at any quiet moment, Harty could be seen sneaking off around the curve of the river to be alone.

They weren't alone at their fire. Their otter neighbours, Devon, Marissa and their children, Stride and Flash, had brought salad and nuts to share. Flash, a strong, athletic female whose real name was Amal, had earned her nickname for her bright and often-seen smile. Her younger brother was called Stride because of his blazing running speed, made evident at such an early age that his parents had long forgotten the name they originally planned to give him. His sister teased this constant whirlwind of activity, saying his original name must have been "Fart with Fur." This usually caused Stride to charge at her, screaming at the top of his lungs with his arms flailing. His sister would flash her wondrous smile and hold him at bay with a paw on his forehead, laughing as clouds of dust rose around Stride's spinning paws.

Pete, the young groundhog and a frequent guest for meals, usually sat next to Silk. His own mother had died the previous autumn after grieving herself sick over the death of Pete's brother a few seasons past. Often lonely, Pete found great comfort sitting around the campfire with Smidge's family. Silk, especially, made him feel at home and, unlike his father, she was a great cook! This meal, rich with flavours of wild spices and loaves of hot bread with meadow butter and honey-dipped desserts, was further evidence of that.

They had all eaten too much. Smidge suggested to Pete an after-lunch trip to the stream to swim and to lie in the sun for a snooze. Pete liked to remind his friend that snoozing was not a problem, but swimming certainly was.

"I am a groundhog . . . *ground*hog! I detest swimming!"

"Yeah, and I can run faster to get the best snoozing spot!" yelled Smidge as he jumped from his log chair and dashed toward the stream.

"Not so fast!" answered Pete, stretching out his paw to trip Smidge, sending him headfirst into a bucket of water. Pete raced ahead, conceding with a yell that Smidge was certainly the first to get wet.

The race was on! Smidge's legs were a blur as he began to overtake Pete. Groundhog legs were stout for digging, but were not built well for speed, and soon the two friends were neck and neck. Down the sandy slope toward the stream they charged. Pete pushed Smidge hard on the back, then abruptly slid to a stop. He laughed as Smidge's momentum caused him to plunge far out into the stream. Panting, the burly groundhog curled up in the sunniest, softest spot on the beach for a snooze.

When Smidge came to the surface, he hollered, "Come on in! The water is beautiful and warm."

"NO! I am still a groundhog. I don't swim," muttered Pete, lying back on the warm sand.

"Well, move over! I am coming in for a landing," warned Smidge as he swam quickly to shore. Swiftly climbing the bank, he used his muscular rear legs to jump high in the air while shaking vigorously. The spray of cold water from his pelt shocked Pete's eyes open just before Smidge landed on the groundhog's plump belly.

"OOOMPH," Pete exclaimed.

Smidge rolled away with tears of mirth running down his cheeks. Then, looking over at his friend, Smidge sensed something was horribly wrong. Pete lay silent and motionless on his back.

"Are you all right?" asked Smidge in a worried tone as he rushed to his friend's side. Frantically, he checked to see if Pete was breathing.

Without warning, Pete forcefully thrust out his stomach, launching Smidge backward. Then he quickly rolled over and pinned Smidge flat, showing absolutely no sign of ill health.

"If I ever want a bath, I'll tell you . . . you . . . water rat!" Pete whispered in a low, angry voice as he moved from atop Smidge.

The two friends lay there in the sun for a long time until, finally, Smidge said in a soft voice, "I am sorry, but since we are friends, maybe you should try swimming."

"Someday," was all Pete said as he turned on his side to face away from his friend.

"Pete, are you scared of the water?" asked Smidge.

Pete did not answer, and they lay there dozing in the sun until Smidge broke the silence.

"I sure hope they tell the story about my dad at the campfire tomorrow night."

"Don't you know it by heart by now?"

"Yeah, but so what?"

"It makes you so sad."

"If only I had been older. I would have fought off those rats, and my father would still be here." Smidge rolled away, hiding his tears. Pete turned on his side, facing Smidge, and rested a heavy digging paw on his friend's shoulder until the sobs stopped and they both fell asleep.

Brookside—Tullymug Woods

Another autumn brought another opportunity to plunder the riches of the harvest gathered by the woodland beasts. Aswar, an enormous rat with a reputation as a fearless warrior, watched the column of rodents march in perfect rank and file—their polished black armour and fearsome weapons glistening in the sunlight. No wonder every beast feared him and his army! Each season, villages were conquered and the survivors, so terrified of another savage attack, gladly agreed to turn over most of their future harvests to King Magnath. This ensured a constant supply of food for the king's fortress without the work. As long as Aswar and his warrior rats remained victorious, King Magnath would be well fed—and happy.

✌

The attack on the peaceful woodland village had started as planned with a swift charge toward the three sides that edged the forest. A meandering brook bound the fourth, and Aswar had hidden archers on the far shore to discourage escape. The village guards had alertly sounded the alarm, but by the time most villagers had taken up their weapons, the rats of Magnath were upon them.

The rapidly approaching sea of black shields and long lances was a terrifying sight for the squirrels and mice, who were taken by surprise while happily bringing in the harvest. The rats' black chest armour and helmets all had the same fearsome emblem— the red serpent and gold sword of Magnath. The villagers had only crude weapons—swords and arrows too light to be useful against King Magnath's well-protected army. Without shields or armour of their own to ward off the fearsome lances and heavy arrows of the rats, the squirrels and mice were vulnerable and ran for cover.

Aswar watched from his vantage point on a rocky outcrop above the settlement as the black tide of rats seemed to swallow the village. He preferred to take the villagers' food and belongings without the lethal violence of combat, but these squirrels and mice were skilled hunters, adept with knives, swords and bows, and they chose to resist.

At the rear of the village stood a large structure made of wooden stakes. Suddenly, its thatched roof flew into the air, thrust upward with long poles by guards hidden inside. From within the walls, twenty archers launched a hailstorm of arrows onto the advancing army. Young ones raced among the archers, delivering more and more arrows so the defenders could fire with maximum speed. But few rats fell, as arrows seldom found the small spaces uncovered by thick armour. The rats continued their advance into the village, their battle cries rising above the crash of sword on sword.

Aswar was relieved to see the black swarm move forward, but quickly became alarmed as a series of desperate counterattacks was mounted. To his dismay, a band of villagers burst forth from beneath a wooden hatch in the ground, immediately behind the main body of his attackers. Nearly a dozen squirrels had been in a storage pit stockpiling the harvest when the attack had begun. Armed with spears, knives and swords, they charged from behind and quickly took down a number of rats.

Seeing his troops in disarray, Aswar feared his soldiers would lose their nerve. Drawing his sword, he charged down the hill directly into the fray. Heads turned as he screamed his war cry, "Magnath!!!" Fighting his way into the midst of his troops, he shouted for the rats to close ranks, turn and oppose the attack from the rear.

Quickly, the tide of the conflict turned in their favour, and Aswar directed his rats to start rounding up the survivors to capture as slaves. He then ran toward a large building that appeared to be the home of the village leader. As he crossed the main village path near a stack of wooden cases, he was ambushed by a squirrel who attempted to cut him in two with a vicious swing of his sword. Countering this squirrel's attack with a lightning motion, Aswar met the blow with his heavier sword. Sweeping his right leg out behind the legs of the villager and bringing his opposite arm forward, he pushed the attacker to the ground. Before the startled beast could rise, Aswar pulled down one of the heavy cases, incapacitating him.

Aswar rushed inside the open door of the hut. There was no sign of the village chief, but two terrified young squirrels cowered in the room's farthest corner. Their crying rose to a deafening din as he approached and extended his paw. Sheathing his weapon, he knelt to their level. Taking pity, he decided he must hide these poor, defenseless youngsters before his troops found them. He rose and searched for a place to conceal them from the pillaging rats. Near the window, he spotted a loose floorboard that he easily pried with his sword to reveal enough space to harbour the two squirrels. As he pushed them into the hole, he warned them in a stern voice to be quiet and quickly replaced the board. Just as he finished, three warriors rushed in. But they pulled up short at the sight of their leader and quickly saluted.

"The battle is won, sir. We were just looking for some . . . er . . . booty . . . sir," panted the tallest through rotting, yellow teeth.

"There is none in here. Bring me the village chief."

"Dead or alive, sir?" asked a short overweight warrior, whose wicked smile revealed a mouth missing most of its teeth.

Before Aswar could answer, the third rat, his face dominated by a wart-covered nose, smirked. "Too late for that, sir. He's deader than a doorknob. Ha ha ha!"

"Fools!" thundered Aswar.

"I didn't do it!" they all rushed to say, backing toward the door as they attempted to distance themselves from their leader's anger.

"Then bring me one of the captives. I'll make sure the villagers understand what happens next harvest season if they don't cooperate."

Regaining some confidence, but still back-pedalling, the tall rat offered, "Not sure we can, boss. Uh, we were sort of too busy to capture anybody."

"Yeah, that's right sir, they took off while we were collecting stuff . . . er . . . for the king," added the fat soldier, food overflowing from its hiding place behind his chest armour.

The three misfits looked at each other, nodding agreement, but all took another step back, crowding into the doorway as they saw Aswar tensing.

Not only were there no slaves to bring to his king, but who would bring in the future harvests of this valley to 'share' with Magnath?

"Greedy idiots!" Striking the flat of his sword on a table-top, Aswar abruptly strode toward the door, eager to leave the bedlam erupting around him. The sounds of arguing and fighting rose in the village as the rats continued their looting rampage. "Tell the rest to gather up what they can and prepare to head back."

Aswar walked to the stream to wash and prepare for the long march back to the mountain fortress of Magnath, where he would accept the judgment of his leader. Would trinkets and a few bushels of grain and nuts be enough to appease the harsh and irrational beast? Or would he die at the whim of the demented king?

3

TALE OF TERRAMBOE

Manorwood

The blazing warmth of a campfire greeted the beasts of the valley and surrounding forest as they gathered for the annual feasting and entertainment that marked the end of the harvest. Chestnuts roasting on the fire sent a delicious aroma wafting through the still evening air. While the young ones ran through the crowd, dodging adults as they played tag, the older beasts engaged in hearty greetings. Some had come from quite a distance to join in the revelry. Long wooden tables arranged near the fire barely supported the weight of the fresh buns and bread, fruit, salads of wild greens, and cider jugs piled upon them.

The squirrel twins, Mash and Dash, and their parents, Misty and Grunch, arrived late, as they had the furthest to come. Their territory lay southeast near the Valley of Stone—a deep rift that cut through Cape Hookross. It was a beautiful place, blessed with calm winds. Clouds of morning mist often formed over the stream winding its way through the bottom of the valley and emptying into the sea off the southern coast of the peninsula. Echoes reverberated eerily off the valley's high walls of stone and caused some beasts to think its thick, dark forest was haunted.

Mash and Dash were named for their blinding speed and fighting abilities. Mash, muscular right down to the tip of his bushy, black tail, loved to wrestle. Dash was slightly smaller and could travel from branch to branch with amazing speed and race over the forest floor with great agility. Despite being full-grown and possessing fearsome physical skills, they remained good-natured and playful. They only visited at harvest-time, so all the young beasts were delighted to see them. Soon, they were deeply involved in a mad game of tag, with everyone trying to catch Dash.

All of the otters had gathered by the fire: five full clans, from babies to white-whiskered great-grandparents. Harnath, the eldest of the otters, was small in stature, but had a mind that remained as sharp as a sword, and his decisions, although made quickly, were usually the best for all. He was a respected leader, and when he stood to speak, the crowd rapidly fell silent.

"Welcome to all. Please enjoy the food, and thanks to those who brought their bounty to share. Once you have filled your plate, find a place by the fire, and let the entertainment begin!"

A small cheer went up, and those who had been busy chatting with old friends moved toward the food. Soon there wasn't a plate left that was not overflowing with selections from the new harvest. Balancing mugs of cider with their heavy plates, young and old surrounded the fire, sitting together on logs or on the ground.

The entertainment was never planned. Names were chosen, and individuals agreed either to lead a song or perform. One and all were fair game! So they all had something prepared, just in case they were called upon.

"Misty and Grunch, sing *The Nut Song*!" yelled out Smidge, causing Mash's and Dash's parents to blush.

Amidst encouraging cheers, Misty and Grunch stood side by side, linked arms and hopped paw to paw as they began to sing:

Chestnuts, walnuts, hazelnuts,
On the ground or in a tree,
Even acorns are nuts you see.

So children, please, do watch your step,
Each nut is precious, yes, you bet!
Please know if you ever steal our nuts
We'll chase you down and tan your butts.

Everyone shouted out their laughter as the two squirrels tossed roasted nuts into the midst of the youngsters. Shrieking with joy the young ones scrambled to gather up the nuts as Misty and Grunch chased after them. As soon as the commotion settled, the crowd chanted for Smidge.

One of Smidge's talents was juggling. His father, Terramboe, had carved three magnificent ash-wood sticks into perfectly weighted juggling props. His mother had found and boiled the plant roots that had yielded the dark purple and red dyes used to decorate the batons.

Smidge rushed inside to unwrap them from their storage cloth and then reappeared, throwing the sticks high into tight, arcing loops. As he approached the fire, the loops arced higher into the night air. As he jumped onto logs and twirled his body in a full circle, he still managed to keep all three sticks flying. Playfully throwing the colourful sticks over Mash's head, he pretended to forget to catch one of them. At the last moment he lashed out his paw to grasp the projectile, just as Mash dove to the ground to avoid being struck.

Amidst loud applause Smidge slowly came to a stop near the edge of the fire so that everyone had a good view of his final trick. Gradually, he threw the sticks higher and higher into the air. Then he suddenly dropped to one knee and skillfully caught the first heavy ash baton and placed it on the ground in front of him. Just as the second stick came hurling to the earth, he twirled and fell backward to nab it and rest it on the ground.

Finally, the stick that seemed to have been launched high enough to touch the stars came whirling down. Smidge, now on his paws, stood perfectly still, his right paw out and his eyes closed. The purple and red stick was turning slowly, end onto end, as its descent grew more visible in the firelight. The sound was sickening as the stick struck Smidge on the top of the head. He fell to the ground senseless.

The crowd groaned. "He's done it again."

"He never gets that one."

"Why does he keep doing that?"

Some of the young children started to cry.

Silk ran over to her son with the cold cloth she had quietly prepared. "My dear son, when are you going to learn?" she whispered. "Now, you won't be able to hear the storytelling."

One eye opened and Smidge murmured, "Oh, yes I will." Then he closed his eyes, and Silk gently stroked his head.

As a distraction, Harnath invited the guests to tell stories or share news. One of the visiting merchants was a mouse, dirty from his travels. He stepped forward, dusting off the front of his satchels.

"Greetings. Enjoy your harvest, for you are fortunate. You do not know the kind of destruction I have seen this season, caused by the rats of Magnath. The weather has been bad in the north, so they are pillaging farther south. Worse yet, there are more slave traders than ever looking for young, strong beasts. So beware. On a lighter note, I will be moving on soon, so hurry up and see me. I have the finest pots and pans in the land."

There was an awkward moment of silence. Smidge's Uncle Gerr sensed the need for a change in the mood of the gathering. He cleared his throat and stood to announce story-time. "It is time for a tale from a harvest of many seasons ago: The Tale of Terramboe, The Mighty One. Gather round and get comfortable."

The children settled on their parents' laps, blankets were drawn about their shoulders and over their legs, and each beast got comfortable in preparation for their favourite story. They had heard it at every harvest, but Gerr's wonderful storytelling voice weaved such magic that they never tired of its recounting. As the tale unfolded, many of the youngsters jumped to their feet to re-enact the attack on the rats. In unison with Gerr, they shouted Terramboe's famous battle cry: "Arise and defend!"

Then, Gerr's voice dropped to a sadder tone. He told the friends and guests seated around the fire how he had watched Terramboe chase the rats into the forest and had lost sight of the brave otter.

"I and many others began to give chase, but arrows flew from the darkness. I was struck in the leg and old Harnath in the shoulder. Those who were able searched the woods, but . . ."

A young voice with a squeak of excitement interrupted Gerr's retelling, causing many to chuckle.

". . . but they never found a trace!"

"That's right, they never found a trace. But thanks to his bravery, the village was safe, and the rats have never returned."

The children erupted into cheers and jumped up, running about wildly and fighting imaginary rats. Smidge, who had recovered halfway through the story, stood at the back of the crowd, listening. Maybe, because he had grown older, his reaction to the tale felt different this time. It wasn't just a story to amuse the children. It was about his long lost father.

Restless, he joined the beasts looking at the merchant's wares. He held in his curiosity until the last of the shoppers wandered away. Then he approached the stranger. "Have you ever heard of Terramboe, my father?"

"The beast in the tale? No, he's probably long dead or a slave in a far-off land. If he was so big and strong, he would have been a prized catch for the slave traders."

"I have never heard of slave traders. Who are they?"

"Deserters of the rat army. They sell beasts to the slave boats or offer them to the evil king in trade for food and safety."

"Have you ever seen them?"

"Sure, but luckily, I am too scrawny. They know they wouldn't get much money for me. Ha ha!"

"Where do you find them?"

"Oh, that's no secret. Go anywhere in the Black Hills, and they'll find you!" With a loud snorting laugh, he packed up the last of his merchandise and began to walk away from the gathering.

Smidge felt a sudden sense of panic and whispered, "Could you take me there?"

The tiny merchant continued walking.

"Never. I am not stupid." Without turning to face him, he dismissed Smidge with a wave of his arm.

Fortress Magnath

Fortress Magnath was perched high in the foothills of the Skull Top Mountains, near the coast. Bounded by the Slave Traders'

Sea to the west and by vast forests to the north and east, it overlooked the coastal foothills and fertile valleys of Hookross Peninsula to the south. On a clear day, the shimmering green and blue of the ocean stretched westward as far as the eye could see.

Moist sea breezes nourished the moss and lichen that blackened the rugged castle's walls of stone. The battlements were enormously thick and high. Besides being a very effective deterrent against attack, the height of the lookout posts provided a commanding view of the surrounding countryside, allowing for easy detection of any approaching beast. Few visitors, friendly or otherwise, managed to make their way to the foreboding fortress, as passages that reached it through the treacherous foothills were scarce.

Legend stated there had been no rats on the peninsula until a ship had brought the black marauders from a faraway land. They had quickly taken advantage of the peace-loving and unassuming local inhabitants, looting villages and taking slaves. The forced labour of generations of slaves had been used to build Fortress Magnath—an unconquerable stronghold that had permitted the rats of Magnath to control the surrounding land without serious challenge for a hundred seasons.

The Kingdom of Magnath was ruled by a long line of despicable and greedy rats, all of whom took the name Magnath when they ascended to the throne. Attaining the throne was often a matter of killing the current king—usually a father or brother.

Waiting for Aswar and his army of black rats to return, Magnath the 13th sat upon a throne decorated with treasures pillaged from victims near and far. The enormous throne had ornately carved wooden arms that extended into the room like dragons' heads. The solid oak back of the throne rose three times higher than the king himself and was topped by a row of spear-headed points. On the upper half of the throne, an intricate pattern of gold and rubies traced the red serpent and golden sword of the crest of Magnath. The thick and expansive plinth of black granite upon which this magnificent throne rose gave the impression that the king ruled from a mountain-top.

On each side of the throne stood three soldiers of the Royal Guard, distinguished by their red tunics with gold trim. The king, trusting no beast, handed out lavish rewards to these chosen soldiers to ensure their 'loyalty.'

Jakbo stood impassively to the side, with his arms across his massive chest. Once the leader of the army, he had been promoted to the position of Commander of the Royal Guard. Despite his age, his hulking presence was still intimidating.

Holding a heavy wooden staff encrusted with multicoloured jewels, the king cast his emotionless black eyes toward the warrior that knelt before him. "Speak of your battle. Leave nothing out," he commanded in a harsh whisper. "I have no time to waste."

Aswar had been summoned upon his return from the battle in the Tullymug Woods to report to the king, with no time to wash or rest. It was always the same. Magnath had to hear a detailed recounting of the battle, which excited him in a strange way. His interest always peaked with the accounting of the loot.

Aswar spoke in a low, controlled manner so no emotion that could possibly anger the king could be detected. He recounted the long journey from the castle through the mountain passes and wooded foothills to the south. The king nodded impatiently as Aswar praised the skill of the trackers who had found the trails the Woodlanders used to forage in the forest. His excitement rose as Aswar described how his army had followed one of these to a ridge overlooking the village to be conquered.

He wished he could have left out description of the battle, but the king wanted every gory detail. Aswar was forced to act out the sword duels, to perform like a court jester, jumping around and brandishing his sword at imaginary enemies. This humiliated and angered every bone in his body, but he knew better than to refuse or fail to look enthusiastic—actions that would send him to the dungeon. The depiction of events always had to end with Aswar pretending to run an opponent through with his sword.

Magnath, excited to the point of agitation by the battle stories, stood to ask about his loot, his eyes wide with anticipation. Aswar embellished as much as he dared, describing the food, tools and trinkets they had brought back. How sad, he thought, that the king and his family would enjoy most of the food and clothing while the slaves would continue to be cold and hungry. With the approaching winter, many of the less hardy would die. Magnath's solution was always to capture more slaves, but this time, Aswar had to admit he had no prisoners. Even worse, no survivors were left behind to bring in next year's harvest.

While the king sat and pondered the news with a scowl, Aswar grimly reflected to himself that at least death had spared the villagers from the hardest, dirtiest chores given to the new slaves. The poor beasts were usually forced to gather firewood outside the protective walls of the fortress in the middle of winter, where the danger was highest and the winds coldest.

"You have done well enough, Aswar, but I am surprised you did not better control the troops. Oh well, it must be very difficult stopping all the killing when they get into a frenzy, eh?" stated the king with a smirk. He had thrown back his heavy black cape and sat restlessly on the front edge of the throne.

Aswar said nothing, but stared coldly into the crazed eyes of the king. *King Crazy the 13th*, he thought.

"You may dine at my table at the feast tonight, but more importantly, you remain alive to serve your king." The mad beast's eyes lost their emotion, and his mood was no longer excited, but cold and indifferent.

"Thank you, my King. If it may please the king, I request to retire to my chambers to wash the soils of battle away so that I may be more pleasant company at your table tonight."

"Dismissed," snorted the king as he abruptly stood and turned, passing through an opening in the thick, red and black tapestry hanging behind his throne. His Royal Guards followed.

Jakbo remained behind and fixed his icy stare upon Aswar.

"Another poor showing." He shook his head with disgust. "You return with less food than last time and no slaves. This never would have happened when I led the army. My spies tell me you are becoming weak and softhearted. You'd better change your ways, or soon you will have outlived your usefulness." He strode from the room, whipping the curtain shut behind him.

Aswar rose stiffly, then turned and walked angrily along the long, red carpet that stretched from the throne to the room's threshold. The clanking of his armour echoed off the high, cold stone ceilings. Safely past the rats guarding the huge, flamboyantly engraved wooden doors, he spat out the foul taste in his mouth. He stepped into the icy fall wind and strode toward his quarters, ignoring the cold and every beast around him. He despised that evil rat. If ever he had the chance, he would dispatch the soulless fool with one mighty swing of his battle-axe.

4

THE SWORD

Brookside—Tullymug Woods

Too scared to even whisper, the two young squirrels lay still, trying to keep their breathing shallow and quiet. While the battle against the black rats raged around them, they had run inside the closest house, hoping to find help or some weapons to defend themselves, but the place had been empty. Moments later, a brutish beast had found them and roughly pushed them into a cramped space under the floor, where they now hid.

Finally, when darkness had come and gone and he had heard no noise for a long time, Alex stirred. He moved first because he had been lying on top of his sister, Marta.

"Come on, let's get out of here."

Marta made no response and remained motionless.

Alex could not move without pressing more heavily upon her. Panicked, he forced up the floorboard and climbed out of the hiding spot. Looking down at her lifeless form, his heart jumped with fear. Had he crushed her? Her face was hard to see in the deepest part of the hole. Maybe she had suffocated.

"Marta, are you all right?" he whispered urgently as he reached down into the dusty hiding place and gently shook her leg.

His heart raced faster when he felt the limpness of her body. He started to pull her out of the hole by her hind legs, dragging her over the rough edge of the wooden floor. He had to brace his paws against a nearby cupboard to gain power as he struggled to raise Marta out of the hiding place. As her shoulders came free, she wheezed loudly, and then deep coughs heaved her chest. With one final tug, Alex slid Marta out of the hole, banging her head hard against the edge of the floor.

"Oh, Marta, I am so sorry," said Alex in a low voice.

"So you should be, you clumsy, mush-brained idiot!" wailed Marta as she rolled over to face her brother. "You squashed my face, and now you hit my head!" she howled, gasping for air.

Alex could not help laughing. "Come on. You're okay, flat-face."

Marta suddenly sat up and spoke urgently, her voice stronger now. "Why is it so quiet? Where is everybody?"

There were no sounds coming through the open window other than the wind and the crackling of flames. The two trembling youngsters slowly crawled to the shutter-less window and raised their heads to look out upon a scene of utter destruction. Tears ran down their cheeks as their eyes moved slowly from one horrible sight to another—overturned carts and burned houses still smouldering, broken dishes and weapons, spent arrows, and worst of all, fallen friends and elders.

They turned and sank to the floor with their backs against the wall, arms around each other, not bothering to wipe away their tears. At campfires, when the elders told stories of ancient battles and recounted glorious acts of heroism and honour, Alex and Marta had wished for the excitement of a conflict. That seemed so naïve and childish now, as they sat surrounded by the grim reality of war.

Marta snapped them back to the immediate problem by suggesting they search for Uncle Spence and see if anyone needed help.

The door, torn off its hinges, lay angled across its frame. Pushing it aside, the two frightened squirrels carefully moved outside. Avoiding fallen boxes and broken plates and bowls, they walked into the smoke.

An outstretched paw protruded from beneath a collapsed table. Marta's face expressed disbelief and sadness as she recognized Simon, her favourite shopkeeper. Simon had a small store filled with the most unusual collection of odds and ends to be found in the entire woodlands, but the best things of all were the jars of chewy candies stored on wooden shelves that stretched from the front door to the back office and reached the ceiling. Their different colours and smells had mesmerized Marta for hours while she tried to make a decision on how to spend the few nuts she had to barter with. Old Simon, always so patient, would wait for her choice of treat and hold out his paw as she slowly counted out the required payment. His smile was forever full and had always made her happy. There was no smile now. Simon looked either angry or surprised; it was difficult to tell. His paw firmly gripped a small sword. He had died fighting—that was certain.

As they wandered, it took some time for them to comprehend the horrors that had taken place. It was hard to believe their village had prospered until only a few hours before. Farming the rich lands around Brookside and harvesting the bountiful offerings of the forest had made their village the envy of many. Every fall, beasts came from far and wide to trade goods, to spend time sharing stories and food, and to sing and dance before continuing on their travels. Now, looted stores with empty shelves, smashed doors and broken hinges stood as the only reminders of that good life.

Alex became angrier with each step he took past tangled heaps of debris, furious with those who had done this to the people he loved, people who meant no harm to anyone. His friends and neighbours had lived in peace with all beasts and had been taught their entire lives that battle weapons were used only for defence—not for hurting anyone in anger.

Eventually tired of walking, Alex and Marta sat on a box turned on its side. Alex scuffed the ground back and forth with his paws.

"We have to do something." His statement sounded more like a question to Marta.

"Like what?"

"Find them. . . . Take revenge!" he shouted, his paws clenched.

"And how are two small Woodlanders going to attack a huge army of horrible rats to seek revenge?" she asked angrily.

"What are we supposed to do, give up?" His reply was equally livid.

The silence between them lasted minutes, but it seemed like hours. The fires around the village were burning out, but wind-blown smoke still stung their eyes.

Finally, Alex spoke softly. "We will find them, but not until we have thought of a plan. We are cleverer than stupid rats, so we can outsmart them, ruin their crops, foul their water, plan ambushes. I don't know, but I am willing to die trying."

Marta did not reply. She did not want to fuel her brother's rage. Soon their thoughts turned to their own immediate survival. When they went to fetch water, they found Uncle Spence's body by the stream with a water bucket in his paw. Now there was no doubt they had to fend for themselves. Solemnly, they undertook the task of filling packs with food scavenged from the burned buildings. Soot covered their paws and faces and darkened their fur until they were almost black. Marta coughed harshly from the smoke hanging in the air, but never stopped searching for anything that might be useful.

Alex was looking for something different. He walked in a trance-like state over burning wood and debris to his uncle's house, where he and Marta had lived since their mother died in the bitter cold of the previous winter. Amazingly, the small wooden building was not as damaged as most houses. The front door was open and everything inside had been thrown helterskelter during the attackers' frenzied search for loot. He peeked into his bedroom, then Marta's, but both were in a shambles. Then he entered his uncle's bedroom and saw that the bed had not been touched except for the bed sheets, which had been thrown on the ground.

Alex knelt at the side of the bed and reached behind the headboard. He felt the coolness of steel and, moving his paw carefully along the metal, he found the handle of his uncle's sword. It felt heavy as he withdrew it from its hiding place, but not as heavy as he remembered it had felt when he tried to lift it as a young child.

Alex had seen the sword only once before, when his Uncle Spence had told him about his days as a warrior. Long ago in the forest, when rats had ambushed villagers gathering food, he and another swords-beast had fought off the attackers, but not before some of the villagers, including Alex's father, had been killed. When Uncle Spence had finished his story, Alex had peeked through the door crack to see where his uncle hid the long, beautiful sword.

Alex shook his head sadly. If Uncle Spence had held his warrior's sword in his paw instead of a stupid water bucket, he may have been able to dispatch those filthy rats.

Slowly, Alex returned to where Marta sat. She looked exhausted and frightened but had packs filled to the brim with supplies. She looked up as he approached and saw the light reflecting off the huge blade her brother carried in his blackened paw.

"What are you going to do with that?" she asked incredulously.

Alex answered sheepishly, "That, I haven't figured out yet."

Fortress Magnath

Aswar sat in a wooden tub filled to the brim with hot water, trying to soak the stiffness out of his tired muscles. He was worried because it was getting harder to find new territory to conquer, which forced his battle-weary troops to travel farther. As well, the Woodlanders were becoming more organized, offering stronger and stronger resistance. No matter how difficult it was to satisfy the insatiable greed of the king, he never seemed content. He forced Aswar to attack again and again and take always more and more, just so the fool could waste it on extravagant feasts and larger statues of himself.

Aswar sighed, dried himself and dressed in his clean, pressed dress uniform for dinner with the king that night. He walked across his sparsely furnished room to its small window and looked up at the glorious night sky. His cramped room reminded him of a prison cell, but the vast sky, filled with bright stars, made him believe there was freedom outside its walls. Before he left, he reached under his bed for a wooden box and pulled out a ragged piece of parchment. He smiled as he ran his finger gently across the ridges made by the paint in the drawing. Someday . . .

∽

The opulence of the great hall was impressive. Every nook and cranny contained objects pillaged during seasons of conquest. The walls were covered with art created by any captured slave who could sew, knit, carve wood or paint. With the handiwork of squirrels, mice, otters and other creatures exhibited, the display was as varied as it was beautiful. The king thought all this made him appear cultured, but to Aswar, it only made him look more like the pretentious, greedy idiot he was.

Loud music meant to encourage a party atmosphere and dancing reverberated off the walls of stone. The musicians were a collection of slaves pulled from their usual mundane drudgery to entertain the king's guests for the evening. Despite the band's questionable musical talent, two spear-carrying guards sat close by to 'encourage them to play.'

Resisting the urge to plug his ears against the racket, Aswar picked his way through the hundreds of guests toward the king's table overlooking the vast room. His Majesty sat surrounded by hangers-on—mostly lower court officials who only survived because they did without question exactly as the king demanded of them. His wife, Queen Gwendolyn, sat at his side, watching the festivities with a blank, resigned look.

Standing rigidly behind the king were his Royal Guards, who looked out of place in the festive atmosphere, but with the king growing more paranoid each day, were always only a spear's length away. Jakbo stood in his usual place to the king's left, scrutinizing the approach of Aswar with his upper lip raised in a slight snarl.

～

Aswar sat beside the queen and looked out over the crowd of army officers, petty government officials and slave guards laughing and enjoying the bounty of food made possible by his recent conquests. For Aswar, there was no joy. His mind was flooded by thoughts of those frightened young squirrels he had hidden to save their lives. At best, they were orphans now; at worst, they had died of thirst and starvation. Sadness filled the fine lines of his face. His shoulders slackened as he settled back into an ornate chair.

"Why so glum, Aswar?" asked the queen, tilting her head slightly toward him.

"I am just tired from a long march, my Lady."

"Balderdash!" she said in a low voice as she moved closer to him. "I have known you for many seasons now and I can see that you are sad."

Aswar glanced at Jakbo, who was watching with suspicion. He often thought the monster was jealous of the attention the queen paid to Aswar. Leaning in, he replied in a quiet voice, "I long for my freedom, a home and a family."

"You know the only freedom my husband plans for you is that obtained through death?"

"Yes, I am very aware."

"That saddens me, Aswar. You are a brave warrior who has fought with honour, despite some of the horrible things that have been asked of you. For that, I feel I owe you. I wear the finest dresses and eat the best food because of you. You are getting older; you don't have much time left. Someday soon I must ask my husband to pardon and release you."

"Save your breath, my Lady. I doubt he would listen, but thank you very much."

"But Aswar . . ."

Before she could continue, he rose to take his leave. "It is no use. His hold over me is too powerful."

None of the revellers noticed his departure. The queen turned back to her husband and nodded, as if she agreed with his every word. But the look in her eyes showed, as usual, that she found whatever he said to be of little importance.

5

THE QUEST BEGINS

Manorwood

S midge awoke upset, with a terrible pain in his head. He remembered the juggling baton arcing beautifully through the night air and . . . well . . . into his forehead, but the real source of his headache was the telling of his father's story. It had made him angry with himself. He felt he had been braver as a little child than now. Why wasn't he doing anything to find his father? He buried his head under his pillow and tried to go back to sleep, but couldn't.

Long ago he had forgotten exactly what his father's face looked like, but he remembered a tall beast with massive shoulders always ready for fun, even after a hard day's work. Smidge missed him so much. He pounded his paw against the side of his mattress, rolled onto his back and studied the shelf above his bed. It had a place for the special things his father had given him—his juggling sticks and the coolest fossil rock that looked like a fish. On the end of the shelf lay the small wooden ball they had used to play all sorts of silly games together. He lay there staring into space and wiping away tears until his reminiscing was interrupted by his mother's voice.

"Stop your wall-a-gag-a-ling and come and have some breakfast."

Moaning, he rolled toward the wall and pulled the pillow over his face. "I don't want any stinking food . . . ever," he spoke softly into his pillow.

The pillow must have muffled the sound of his mother's paw-steps, for the next thing he knew, it was whipped away and he was suspended in the air. Hanging from his mother's strong right paw by the scruff of his neck, he faced the wagging index finger of her left paw. The motion came so close to his face that his eyes crossed, making his headache worse.

"There is no time to lie around in bed feeling sorry for yourself because your juggling trick didn't work. There is work to be done and I can't be expected to do it all!" Her face seemed to enlarge and contract, filling his vision as he swung back and forth in her grip. She was mad!

"I wasn't sad about that. I missed the beginning of Uncle Gerr's story about Dad. That's why I'm sad."

"Smidge, you have heard that story enough times to bore a sloth. Your father is long gone, likely dead. I miss him too, very much, but we have to move on. We won't survive another season if we don't have food to eat or firewood to keep us warm! Do you understand, Smidge? Do you?"

"I hate it when you say he's dead. He's not dead. He's trying to get home to us. We have to remember him." As he spoke, he burst into sobs. Silk lifted her son's chin with her paw so they could make eye contact, and her tone softened. "We aren't forgetting him. We never will, but he would want us to be strong and take good care of each other and not waste precious time lying in bed feeling sorry for ourselves." As she spoke, she gradually pulled him to her chest, sat down on the bed and hugged him tightly.

"You never told me about slave traders. Maybe he didn't die in the forest. He could be alive, a slave somewhere." Smidge suddenly pushed away and stomped down the stairs. His heavy paw-steps on the stairs echoed in Silk's ears as she remained on the bed. She folded her paws across her chest and hugged herself for a second. *What difference does it make?* she thought. With a sigh, she brushed away tears from her cheeks with her strong, calloused paws before she rose to go back to work.

Smidge didn't stop for breakfast. He stormed outside and crossed the yard. Upon entering the storage shed, he waited for his eyes to adjust to the dim light and then reached toward the top shelf, probing. His paws finally found packages of nuts and dried fish wrapped in salt cloth. He moved over to the next set of shelves and selected packets of hard bread and cheese. Searching in the darkness, he found an old burlap sack to carry the provisions. He tied a knot and pulled the string tight, using the long end of the string as a handle to hoist the sack up over his shoulder. Cautiously, he peered out the doorway. When he was sure no one was coming, he stepped out into the morning sun and started walking briskly towards the woods. His heart leapt into his mouth at the sound of Pete's loud voice coming from behind him.

"Where are you going, wandering around outside with a dirty sack over your shoulder?"

"None of your business," retorted Smidge as he quickened his pace.

"I am your friend. You look upset and . . . you are acting rather strangely. So I want to know what is going on," replied

Pete, his voice tinged with anger. "Anyway, I thought otters slept in bathing suits."

"Well, what are you doing, snooping around my house when you could be lying in a pile of dirt somewhere? Now leave me alone and pretend you never saw me."

"It's sort of hard to forget an otter in his pajamas, carrying a sack of food. Maybe, before you leave to go wherever it is you are going, you should put on some clothes," suggested Pete with a smile.

Pete had not come to see his friend without reason; he knew exactly what Smidge was doing. It was predictable. Every time The Tale of Terramboe was told, Smidge talked about running away to find his father. Usually, he left the front door of his house and came in the back door within ten minutes. The older Smidge got, the more serious his efforts seemed to become, and the farther he ventured. Smidge finally stopped walking away and waited for his friend with a determined look in his eyes.

Pete moved closer to him and asked softly, "Why this time?"

"After talking to that travelling merchant . . . I don't know . . . I just think he's alive. Besides, I am old enough now to go and find him. I am leaving this time . . . for real!" Smidge said emphatically, the whole time shifting from paw to paw and scuffing the ground. "After I change, be ready to come if you want to." He abruptly turned, slid the sack back into the shed, and walked toward his home.

Pete didn't have to think long. "Might as well, 'cause there is nothing better to do!" And he hurried home to pack.

The Tullymug Woods

Danger. Fear. That was all Marta could sense. Her shoulders felt heavy and her eyes wouldn't open. She struggled to rise but could not. The morning light entered her half-open eyes as she drifted back and forth between sleep and wakefulness.

Trudging along the deep woodland trail toward the next village while carrying such heavy packs had been a hard day's work. Marta and Alex had never ventured out of their village before! Based on recollections of stories recounted by the many travellers who passed through their community, they had headed in the direction they agreed must take them to the nearest town. Then, exhausted from the long walk away from the burning village, they had slept at the side of the woodland path, sheltered by thick bushes.

Marta had fallen asleep instantly, dreams racing through her mind all night. But she had found this last dream terrifying and it wasn't going away! Every time she tried to change position on the lumpy ground, the sensation remained: a dirty, smelly paw pushing down on her chest. Finally, she swung her arm against it . . . it was hard, really hard. It was real!

Before she could fully awaken and react, the tip of a sword was pushing painfully on her throat with a pressure so suffocating that she couldn't even squeak out her brother's name. When her vision finally cleared, all she could see was one bloodshot eye staring down at her. A rat stood above her, his yellow teeth forming a crooked smile upon a dirty, lopsided face. Unable to move her head without inflicting more pain from the sword tip, she twisted her eyes to the last spot she remembered seeing Alex. She couldn't move her eyes far enough to see him, but a scratchy, high voice came from his direction.

"I got a snivelling youngster here. What you got, Jimmy?"

"Nothin', Slim. Just a girl without enough jewellery to make it worth our while to rob her," drawled the foul-smelling, one-eyed rat in a low, gruff voice. A large scar ran up the side of his face until it disappeared under a black eye patch covering his right eye. His tattered, faded tunic was deeply stained with filth.

"Well, they're too tiny for slaving, so we best just kill 'em and take their food," answered Jimmy's accomplice nonchalantly. He was as ugly as his partner, but with a dirty eye patch over his left eye.

That was it! These didn't look like the rats that had laid waste to her village, but they were still rats! Rats like those who had killed her father and Uncle Spence. With a sudden explosion of anger, Marta kicked as hard as she could, striking the rat named Jimmy behind the knee. The rat's leg buckled, but he recovered and fiercely returned his sword to his victim's throat.

With the distraction, Alex wiggled a paw free and hit Slim with enough force that the surprised rat lurched sideways. This allowed enough time for Alex to raise himself on one arm and leg. As he rolled, he reached under his sleeping mat and grabbed his uncle's sword. Thrusting the mighty weapon upward, he inflicted a gash in the rat's thigh. Slim stumbled away into the bushes, screaming and clutching his wound.

Rising, Alex launched himself at Jimmy, who had Marta pinned down. But, the rat jumped off Marta and dodged sideways. Alex's momentum carried him over Marta and he landed with such impact, the sword was dislodged from his paw.

Now free, Marta reacted swiftly. She rolled over and quickly grabbed the fallen weapon. Alex, catching his wind, turned back to see Marta standing, facing the ugly scum. His weapon on the ground, Jimmy stood with his arms held high in surrender but with a smirk on his hideous face.

Marta stood defiantly with Uncle Spence's sword poised over her head, but as she turned her gaze to check on Alex, her arms froze in mid-air. The look on her face turned to panic. With his arm painfully jerked backward, Alex lay pinned to the ground by the wounded Slim, who had circled back through the bushes.

Seeing Alex incapacitated, Jimmy relaxed, winked his good eye and sneered at Marta, "Drop the sword, girlie, before Slim cuts your friend's throat."

Slim crouched behind the helpless squirrel. As he pulled himself closer, with his sword drawn tightly across Alex's neck, the foul stench of his rotting teeth blew hot air across Alex's face.

"Thought you'se was clever did you? Well, think again! Ha ha ha!"

"No! You think again, you scum!" screamed Marta as she turned and flung herself sideways at the rat threatening Alex.

Driving her shoulder into Slim's upper body, she knocked the beast flying.

Left unguarded, Jimmy recovered his sword and charged toward Alex, now sword-less. The young squirrel scrambled to get away, but one of the wild swings of the rat's sword cut deeply into his flank, and Alex lay back with a heavy moan.

Brandishing his sword with two paws, Jimmy now charged toward Marta. Although stumbling to regain her paws, Marta thrust her sword upward, striking the onrushing Jimmy in the belly. The stunned rat staggered backward.

Meanwhile, Slim had nimbly jumped to his paws, poised to attack, with his rusty blade held high. Marta leapt forward to counter him. The two combatants stood face to face, drawing huge, misty mouthfuls of air and gasping from their exertion.

Nervously facing the fierce young squirrel with the imposing sword, Slim screamed a piercing stream of foul language, ending with, "Help, Jimmy! Where in the heck are you?"

There was no reply for a long time, but then a pitiful sound broke the silence. "The fight gone and left me, it has," moaned

Jimmy, slumped against a tree stump. The one-eyed rat looked dreadful lying in the dirt clutching the blood-soaked fur on his belly.

Slim, taken aback by the wretched wailing, moved backward in retreat. Then he turned and ran toward his partner, but as he passed a nearby tree trunk, he pushed off with one leg, launching into a somersault. Landing beside Marta, he slashed at her neck. The acrobatic move surprised Marta, but reflexively she recoiled from his rusty blade, falling backward. Hearing her brother's pained cries, her glance was temporarily drawn toward Alex, who lay clutching his stomach, his complexion white as winter frost.

Slim, seeing that Marta was distracted, ran toward her with his sword raised in feverish anticipation of a kill. Arching his back, he began a mighty downward swing at Marta's head.

Kicking toward the oncoming rat, Marta managed to strike his right leg below the knee with enough force to throw off his aim. Sparks flew as his sword struck the rocky ground beside her with a fearsome sound. Lying on her back, Marta swung with all her might at the rat's other leg, cutting the back of his ankle. The screeching rat fell to his knees and rolled onto his side, clutching his wound.

Marta rose and stood over the pathetic, dirty creature with her sword raised to strike. "I'll spare you, but you and your friend are never to bother Marta the Marauder again, or you die. Now move, get lost, fast!" She pointed to the forest with her free paw.

Despite their wounds, the two rats scrambled to their paws and painfully made their way into the forest. Slim turned to stare coldly at Marta and spit defiantly on the ground before he limped into the shadows.

"Can you walk, Alex?'

"I think so. Help me up."

Supporting her wounded brother, Marta looked back toward the woods to make certain that the disgusting rats had not returned. She picked up their knapsacks, and they slowly shouldered them and resumed their journey.

"Well, what do you think of that sword now, Marta? Sorry, I should say 'Marta the Marauder,'" grinned Alex.

"Quite useful," was all she said. She was preoccupied, scouring the path ahead for trouble.

☙

As they walked, Alex seemed to get heavier on Marta's arm. Finally, he stumbled so badly he fell, pulling Marta on top of

49

him. Marta used her free paw to pull him back up, but as she did so she felt a warm, sticky wetness on his fur. She looked into his face and saw only a pale ghost of her brother.

"Oh, Alex," she murmured. "We have to get you some help."

She guided him to a hollow filled with dry leaves, rested his back against a fallen log and covered him with a small, woven blanket from her pack. Gingerly, she held the water container to his lips. He weakly slurped some liquid and then let his head fall back against the mossy surface of the log behind him. His eyes closed and his body went limp as he fell unconscious.

Marta turned and looked in her pack for something to make bandages. "What are we going to do now?" she asked herself, with tears flowing down her cheeks.

Manorwood

Gerr sat on a log by the fireside with his arm around Silk while she sobbed. Smidge was nowhere to be found. Despite his looking, there had been no sign of his nephew. Even Harty, who usually didn't pay much attention to his young nephew, had volunteered to search by swimming along the river. Clearly, this was not one of the young rascal's minor excursions, because it was well past dinner-time and he had not yet returned. Usually, the minute he became hungry he reappeared to explain how he had lost track of time, or had been waiting for Pete, or to offer some other excuse for his lateness.

While Gerr had been searching the edge of the meadow, he had met Pete's father, Ralph, also looking for his missing son. Returning to Manorwood, the two of them now were resting, exhausted from their all-day search.

Agitated, Silk slipped from beneath Gerr's arm and stood to face him. "What worries me, Gerr, is how upset he was this morning. I think this time he is determined to find his father."

Ralph spoke up. "Yes, with Pete missing too, you could be right. Pete has often mentioned the possibility of joining Smidge in a search for his father. Silk, you say there is food missing from the pantry? Pete wouldn't go anywhere without a ton of food."

"Food? Yes. Enough for a long trip. And Smidge's pack and knife are gone from under his bed," replied Silk. She stopped her restless pacing and abruptly dropped onto a log as if all her energy had suddenly departed. "I can't lose them both," she cried softly.

"We'll form a search party to start in the morning, and when we find him I'll let him have a piece of my mind!" Gerr responded sternly.

"Indeed. They won't be going on any crazy adventure again once we are through with them," Ralph added.

Silk wiped tears from her face and spoke softly under her breath, "It's not crazy . . . just dangerous." Her sobbing started anew and, rising quickly, she disappeared into her hut.

"What did she say?" asked Gerr.

"I think she said we are courageous," said Ralph, scratching his head.

Gerr knew Silk was suffering doubly: first she had lost her husband, and now she was in danger of losing her son. Eager to get going, he rose to his paws. "Let's call a clan meeting."

"After dinner?" suggested Ralph.

"No, now!" said Gerr impatiently, as he hurried off to spread the word and find volunteers for the search party.

The Valley of Stone

Smidge and Pete had walked most of the day, and the shadows of the late afternoon sun were rapidly lengthening as they headed east into the Valley of Stone. There, a twisting, narrow path cut steeply through the rocks of the gorge, taking the two beasts deeper into the darkness. The sounds of stones dislodged by their paw-steps echoed off the dark granite walls, bombarding their ears with the noise.

Pete, always steady on his paws, led the way over the loose stones, with Smidge resting a paw on his back to keep his balance. The echoes were spooky, and Smidge constantly twisted his head from side to side, checking for threats. Not watching his paws, he tripped, knocking down Pete and landing heavily on the unsuspecting groundhog. The two friends slid down the rocky path to a bumpy stop. Caught beneath Smidge, Pete squirmed, clutching his bottom and yelping with pain.

"Get off of me, you crazy, dried-out otter. Has not being in the water all day caused your sponge brain to dry up and shrivel?"

A piercing, howling sound erupted from above them and reverberated along the valley. Smidge frantically scrambled to his paws, but stumbled and fell, landing heavily on his back. Sliding in the loose gravel, he crashed into Pete just as the groundhog was trying to get to his paws. Another loud howl cut through the air. Pete screamed with fright as he tumbled and slipped downhill on his belly. The two friends came to rest in a jumble against a tree trunk. Two beasts landed beside them, howling shrilly and then doubling over with laughter. "What in the heck are you guys doing—summer tobogganing?"

Smidge rolled to his knees and brushed himself off. "Mash and Dash, you jerks. That wasn't funny! You nearly scared me out of my fur!"

"We were just having a little fun," laughed Dash.

"What are you doing here, anyway?" asked Mash, helping Pete to his paws.

Smidge stood and picked up his sack. "We are on a quest to find my father."

Mash and Dash looked at each other, unsure of what to say. "Don't you think maybe your dad is . . . well . . . dead?" asked Mash.

"I know he's not. I can feel it in my heart, and besides, even if he is, I owe it to him and my mother to at least try to find out what happened," said Smidge softly.

The four friends stood silently for a moment before Dash broke the tension with a welcoming gesture. "Well, then, you guys want to come to our place and have supper after your long walk?"

Pete, who was never shy about food, stated that would be wonderful and immediately began to walk along the path.

༄

The two squirrel brothers nimbly led the travellers down the steep, rocky trail into the forest that covered the valley floor. They crossed a wide stream atop an enormous log, looking down at white-water rapids cascading over rocks and boulders that had collected during many seasons of rockslides.

Eventually, they came to a clearing that contained the tallest tree Smidge and Pete had ever seen. The soaring oak tree had a trunk so great, it had to be hundreds of seasons old. Huge limbs forked outward about twenty feet above the ground, providing support for a structure of mud, grass and sticks that was the squirrels' home. The enormous dwelling stretched across one side of the big tree to the other. Lookouts punctuated the structure at intervals, and a large thatched door dominated the main wall.

The squirrels and Smidge effortlessly began climbing up the tree. Fortunately for Pete, the oak also had smaller branches and contours to allow him to slowly make his way upward. The squirrels' surprised parents, Grunch and Misty, were warmly greeting the other three as Pete huffed through the front door.

"Nice house, but it would be even nicer if it was on the ground, or even under it," complained the tired-looking groundhog.

"Well, you lads must be starving! Come sit at the table. We were just about to eat," welcomed Misty.

℘

The meal tasted absolutely fantastic, and the two travellers were eating great quantities very quickly. Pete, always a vigorous eater, was outdoing himself. Although Misty was pleased that the food was being enjoyed, everyone could see her wince at the sound of Pete's lips slurping and smacking.

"Pete, are you trying to eat the spoon too?" laughed Grunch.

"My, it is good to see a young beast enjoy his food," commented Misty, as she made another trip to the kitchen to fill up the serving bowls again.

A loud "Burrrrrp . . . bluuuuup" erupted from Pete's mouth as he began to speak. "This is the best food I've eaten in a long time! I think I like climbing trees after all. I especially hate climbing down trees, so I guess I'll be able to taste this wonderful food for quite awhile."

A look of horror briefly passed through Misty's eyes, but she chuckled and hastily recovered. "Why, I can certainly pack some food for you to take on your journey home," she suggested, choosing to ignore Pete's request to move into the tree fortress.

"It is wonderful you lads paid us a visit," interjected Grunch happily.

Even with his mouth full of delicious food, Pete was eager to socialize. "We are on a quest to find Terramboe!" Ignoring a firm kick from Smidge, he carried on. "We are heading north . . ."

"Pete and Smidge, are your parents okay with this?" interrupted Grunch.

"My mother understands," replied Smidge firmly.

Smidge glanced toward Pete with a conspiring look, but before the groundhog could add his reply, Misty spoke firmly.

"Not so quickly. Smidge, you didn't really answer Grunch's question about your mother giving permission."

Not waiting, Grunch continued. "I would be very worried about your safety. The Black Hills to the north are filled with robbers and slave traders. Not to mention the roving rat army of Magnath, which is always on the lookout for beasts to do their dirty work. I am sorry, but I can't let you continue. In the morning, Mash will escort you back toward Manorwood."

"What about me?" Tears were welling in Dash's eyes.

"You will stay here with your mother and me. You have chores to do. There will be no further discussion of this."

Dash abruptly left the room.

Mash rose with a smug smile on his face. "I will show you to your bedrooms, since we have a big day ahead of us."

With that, the three young beasts hurriedly left for the bedrooms. Pete and Smidge were fast asleep before Grunch and Misty had the kitchen cleaned up.

6

SPARKS AND SNAKES

The Valley of Stone

After a hearty breakfast, Smidge, Pete and Mash headed out on the path toward Manorwood. Pete burped and farted with each paw-step, especially on his way up the steeper portions of the trail. Initially, his companions had laughed. Now, they walked well ahead of him.

"Wait up. I can't help it if your mother is such a good cook. It's just a little indigestion, that's all."

"More like a lot of indiscretion, you dirt bag," replied Mash.

At the stream, they waited for Pete to catch up. After giving the groundhog a minute to rest, Smidge started across the giant log they had crossed the day before.

But Mash grabbed the otter's arm and pulled him back. "I left my parents a note," he said.

"That's sweet. Now let's go! My mother is going to get madder every minute I am gone."

"Listen, it says I am going with you."

"Duh, yeah," chimed Smidge and Pete.

"On the quest, you losers. I know you aren't going home."

"What? We are so. Right, Pete?"

Pete looked puzzled, then smiled. "Yeah, home by lunch."

Mash rose impatiently. Walking along a path away from the stream, he asked over his shoulder, "Do you guys even know which direction north is?" Without waiting for an answer, he continued on. "I'll show you."

The Tullymug Woods

Marta pulled Alex along the path on the blanket, dust billowing up after them. She wasn't sure where she was headed, but after a night of listening to her brother moaning and talking delirious nonsense, she had to keep moving. Surely, they would come to a settlement along the way. Walking kilometre after kilometre without seeing a soul, she realized how little she really knew about anything outside of their little village. She had just assumed that the world would be filled with wonderful places like theirs, surrounded by deep forests and rich with food, warm cosy homes, and green pastures to play in. This other world felt lonely, and danger seemed to lurk around every corner. Coughing from the dust blown toward her by the strong wind, she dragged Alex to the side of the path. Sitting on a log to rest, she felt alone, lost and very nervous. Shivers ran up and down her spine when she remembered those two evil rats that had attacked them. Where the courage had come from to fight back remained a mystery to her.

Deep in thought, her heart stopped for a second when she heard a sound further along the path. She quickly tucked the edges of the blanket around Alex and pushed him into the bushes. Rolling over the log to hide, she became caught on the remains of a branch on its far side. Although upside down she lay still, trying not to make a sound.

A mouse approached, walking swiftly along the path and carrying a huge bundle suspended on a long wooden pole hoisted over his shoulder. Dangling from his pack and from leather straps over his other arm was an amazing array of pots and pans, spoons, tools and wooden bowls. His voice seemed too big for his body as he sang.

> *Oh my, 'twas a wonderful day.*
> *Filled with joy I ran out to play,*
> *But then came down the pouring rain*
> *Soaked me wet and made me sad again!*
> *"Don't cry," is what my Momma did say,*
> *"Cause every day's a beautiful day*
> *In the land of milk and honey,*
> *To stay inside and count your money!"*

The mouse was singing his song at the top of his lungs. Frequently, because he closed his eyes to hit the highest notes, he stumbled over rocks in the path. The packs draped over his shoulders were tattered and dirty, as though he had been travelling for a long while. Yet happiness seemed to spread out around him in waves as he quickly moved past Marta.

Thinking that a beast singing such a cheerful song couldn't be too dangerous, she called out, "Hey, mister!"

The mouse must have jumped a foot in the air with surprise. Sliding the sack off the wooden pole with a loud clatter of pots and pans, he brought the stout ash branch up as a weapon. Dismayed when he could not see who had spoken, he twirled around and around on the path.

"Who said that? Where are you? Show yourself!"

Marta wiggled wildly, trying to free herself, but in vain.

The mouse, sensing movement behind the log, approached it slowly, raising the staff into a threatening position. All he could see was a brown-coloured object bobbing slowly near the log at the side of the path. Not sure if it was a dancing mushroom or some strange creature about to attack, he brought his staff down with all his might. His blow struck the log, knocking off loose bark. Anticipating a counterattack, he jumped backwards but fell over his sack lying in the path.

The force of the blow had broken the branch suspending Marta, and she fell to the ground, striking her nose and inhaling dirt.

"Ouch, what whid yoo whoo dat for?" Marta sputtered, spitting out a mouthful of dirt and leaves. "I need help, not a spanking!" Picking herself up, she approached the mouse, who was desperately crawling backward, trying to get away. While wiping the dirt from her face, she demanded, "Who are you?"

The mouse rose on his foot paws and made a show of stretching to his full height and puffing out his chest. "Spit."

"I did already. I am fine. Now, WHAT IS YOUR NAME?"

"Spit!!!"

"What?" questioned Marta, thinking she had misheard.

"They call me Spit!" he growled in a loud voice, scuffing his paw angrily on the ground.

"Why in the world would they call you Spit?" Marta asked, trying to quell her agitation.

Suddenly, with a loud horking sound and a forceful heave of his shoulders, a large gob of spit came hurling out of the little mouse's mouth and landed close to Marta's paws.

"Yuck!" she exclaimed, stepping back and almost falling over the log again. "That's disgusting!"

"Disgusting to you, but I can knock the stinger off a bee at twenty paces!" he said defiantly. He dusted himself off, gathered his trinkets and started to move away, down the path. "So now you know why they call me Spit, lady."

"Wait! I need help. My brother is injured. I see you are a travelling merchant. Do you have any medicine or bandages?" she pleaded, chasing after him.

The little ragtag merchant slowed his pace but without looking back, muttered, "Maybe." He walked several more paces and suddenly stopped, causing Marta to bump into him. "Do you have money? I am no Good Samaritan, you know."

Marta's hopes sank but she quickly recovered. "I have goods to trade," she offered. "I have food. Good food and . . . and . . ." She was becoming desperate as Spit shrugged his shoulders and kept walking away. "I have a beautiful sword!"

That worked! Spit turned quickly, a sly smile on his face. "Now you're talking, lady!"

Northeast of the Valley of Stone

Smidge and Pete were following Mash along a rough path through a forest of tall white pines. The three friends had been travelling for many hours.

Even though it was not Mash's father they were looking for, Mash loved adventure. A little older than the other two, he had eagerly taken on a leadership role and was proving to be a tough taskmaster. He was setting a fast pace.

"Can't we find a river soon? I really need a swim!" complained Smidge.

"I'd like to lie down in a dark, cool den and sleep," added Pete.

Mash's voice dripped with sarcasm. "I'd like to swing from tree to tree with my face stuffed full of acorns . . . you snivelling softies! What kind of questing heroes are you?"

"Tired ones!" replied Pete and Smidge in unison.

"Not much further, lads! Just ahead there is a good camping spot near a river where we can settle in for the night. Then, in the morning, we aren't far from the main path to the Black Hills. Come on, pick up your paws!"

Tullymug Woods

Spit dressed Alex's wounded side with large bandages from one of his many packs. First, he had gone deep into the forest to gather leaves and roots, spending time searching for just the right ones. Vigorously pounding and stirring, he had made a thick poultice of herbs and root paste to spread over the gash. When he applied the mixture, he became worried about the depth of the wound and the signs of infection around the edges. Muttering to himself, he returned to the woods and found leaves from a reddish fern to add to the concoction. Tearing strips of bandages, he bound the wound tightly, commenting that the lad was lucky to be alive. Finally satisfied with his work, he wrapped up his supplies and packed everything away.

"Well, miss, I have done as you requested. Now I would appreciate payment in full." Holding out his paw, he eyed the magnificent sword leaning against Marta's pack.

"Not so fast, Mister Spit. Certainly, you wouldn't leave us lost in the forest!"

Edging toward the sword with his arm outstretched, the bold hawker replied, "I am in a hurry, for it is a very busy season. With the harvest coming in, customers are in a buying mood."

He lunged for the sword, but Marta had grabbed it first, and with lightning speed, poised it at the mouse's throat. The little mouse showed not a bit of fear, for equally as quickly he had drawn a small knife, which he held to Marta's stomach.

He smiled slyly. "Well, well, dear, I may have underestimated you—and you, me. Let us put down our blades now, thank you. Certainly, we can work out a mutually acceptable deal."

After a very brief negotiation, he reluctantly agreed to guide them to the nearest settlement, and off they went. Hours went by as Spit expertly guided Marta through the many choices of paths and Marta pulled Alex on a blanket behind her. While Spit walked merrily along, singing his annoying little ditties, Marta could feel her legs getting heavier and her breathing strain. With great effort, she pushed each paw in front of the other and hoped that she was right to trust this despicable, greedy little mouse. However, for all her worrying, she had not come up with any alternative.

Suddenly, on a downhill slope, Marta's shoulders were wrenched backward as Alex's blanket caught on something in the path. Too tired to steady herself, she started to fall toward her brother. Not wanting to land on Alex, she then lunged forward as hard as she could, trying to wrestle loose. The blanket tore away and she shot forward without it. Exhausted and unable to control her speed, she gathered momentum, her legs moving faster and faster as they carried her down the incline. Paws outstretched to break her fall, she went whizzing past Spit.

Spit stood back from the cloud of dust rising from Marta as she shot past him on the path. Incredulous, he exclaimed,

"What's the rush, lady?" And then, turning to see Alex's motionless body left behind on the blanket, "Your brother isn't going to catch up!" Laughing heartily at his own joke, he watched Marta trip on a rock, slide off the side of the path, lose her pack and begin tumbling. He followed her path and got to the riverbank just in time to see the strong current pull a motionless Marta into its grasp. She feebly splashed the water with her paws until the current swept her away.

Climbing back to where Alex lay on the blanket in the middle of the pathway, Spit muttered, "Don't look at me. I am not pulling you." Since there was no helping the girl, and it appeared her brother would live, Spit felt no obligation to stay.

Eager to resume his business, he looked back from the steep edge of the path and spoke to the oblivious Alex.

"Sweet dreams. Your sister is certainly on the move, but you're a real drag!" He chuckled and added, "If you think I am sticking around, you *are* dreaming. I am out of here."

To emphasize his statement, he let loose a large spitball onto the dusty path, then headed down to Marta's pack and slipped out the beautiful sword. Puffing out his chest now, he strutted along the trail, kicked up dust with his paws and sang:

Away I go
To carry on my way,
Never to stay
Nor waste a day
That I can make
Lots of moneeeeey!

❧

Although farther away than Mash had led them to believe, the camping spot by the river proved to be excellent. Previous travellers had left behind a well-made fire pit formed of smooth river stones, and an ample supply of kindling and logs protected by a covering of bark pieces sat ready for use.

Smidge found the warm fire welcoming after his long dip in the cool river. Pete, not about to go swimming, was curled up in a ball, snoring loudly by the warm stones around the pit. Famished, Mash rummaged through a knapsack for supplies to make dinner.

"Wake up, Pete! Since you don't do much else but eat, you are elected cook!" shouted Smidge, as he prodded his friend's bristly side. "Rise and shine, or there will be no food to eat."

Pete propped himself up against the log behind him. "No food? What are you talking about?" He said groggily.

"Pete, why don't you go and wash up so you can cook us dinner?" said Smidge, pointing to the river. "You can get water and . . . hey, what the heck is that in the river?!"

"I don't know, but it is a drowning *something.*"

"Come on. Let's go!" cried Mash, as he leapt over Pete and joined Smidge, who was already running to the riverbank.

The three companions worked in unison to bring the lifeless form to shore. At first, Pete had frozen, staring intently at the river, but then had ventured knee-deep into the icy water to help. Smidge, who had used his powerful swimming muscles to propel the drowning victim across the forceful current into the waiting paws of his friends, collapsed on the rocks, gasping for air. Mash pushed and Pete pulled, slipping and sliding on the wet stones as they frantically fought to bring the creature to safety. Finally, they succeeded in getting the limp, sodden shape onto shore and then up onto a flat, grassy ledge.

"It's a squirrel girl!" exclaimed Mash, once they had gently placed Marta on the grass.

"And a dead one if we don't do something quick!" replied Pete. "We have to get the water out of her lungs. Turn her over."

Fumbling urgently, Smidge and Mash turned the drowned squirrel onto her front.

Promptly, Pete lay on her back with his heavy chest. Seeing no response, he raised himself on his front legs and let his weight fall heavily on the squirrel.

"What are you doing? You'll crush her!" cried Mash. "What do you know about drowning?"

"Everything! I am a groundhog who can't swim."

"So?" Mash angrily pulled on Pete's shoulders to pry him away.

Pete's powerful shoulders wrestled free, and he let his chest fall heavily on the lifeless squirrel again. "I've seen this before, now let me . . ."

As he was speaking, the girl gave a large cough, and a gush of water sprayed into Smidge's face. Pete jumped away and pushed her onto her side. For what seemed like an eternity, they waited for her to take a breath. With a sudden forceful effort, the creature gasped an enormous gulp of air, followed by a long coughing fit punctuated with more rapid breaths.

"Are you all right?" asked Mash anxiously as he knelt down.

Slowly, one of the pretty young squirrel's eyes opened, and in a soft voice she murmured, "Peachy keen, what do you think?"

Shocked silence hung in the air for a second before Smidge and Pete broke into roars of laughter and sighs of relief.

Mash was speechless, but slowly a grin came to his face. "I am glad," was all he said as he continued to study her face.

"Hey, Mash, look alive. Stop staring like you've never seen a girl before!" teased Smidge. "She's going to freeze if we don't get her over to the fire."

Marta had closed her eyes and begun to shiver.

Mash quickly scooped her up into his powerful arms and rushed toward the warmth. "Well, you two laughing hyenas better put some wood on that fire and heat water for tea! Hurry up!"

"Yes sir!" the friends replied with mock formality and salutes as they ran behind.

Mash cleared a spot near the fire and placed Marta gently on the ground, her head resting on a packsack. After wrapping her in all the blankets they possessed, Mash joined his friends as they gathered wood and stoked the blaze.

"Hey, Pete! I can't believe you got wet!" cajoled Smidge.

"I can. I just don't like it."

"Well, anyway, thanks. You were a big help."

ა

Marta did not remember much of the next few hours, but she sensed the comfort of the muscular squirrel's arms carrying her, the sounds of the friends bantering and the warmth of the roaring fire. Later in the night when the fire's heat began to wane, she awoke, shivering. Beneath the mound of blankets that had been thrown over her, she raised herself onto her side and studied the sleeping figures around the fire. Her head felt fuzzy and she struggled to understand where she was.

A very well fed groundhog slept on his back, snoring loudly, with his paws swaying in the air. Occasionally, his legs would engage in some activity, perhaps tunnel digging, and dreamy murmurs would interrupt the snores. The otter was lean and strong-looking but not yet an adult. He slept soundly as though he hadn't rested in days. Finally, a young squirrel lay propped up against a log, sleeping lightly, often blinking and trying to open his eyes. His paw hovered over a knife tucked into a large belt around his waist. He appeared to be the leader and a handsome leader at that.

As Marta moved to sit up, Mash awoke with a start, firming his grip on the knife. "Oh, you're awake. You fell asleep before you could drink the hot tea we made you."

"Hello, I am Marta and you . . . ?"

"Oh, sorry, I am . . . um . . . Mash from the Valley of Stone," he replied. For some reason, he felt very nervous speaking to this girl.

"I am not sure I remember how I got here, but thank you, and yes, I would like some tea now."

"Oh yes, yes, but it might be cold, and the fire needs tending."

Mash jumped to his paws, grabbed some wood and tossed it on the fire, spraying a few sparks into the air. Quickly testing the tea, he found it lukewarm and pushed the water pot over a hotter part of the flame.

"It will be just a moment to boil more water. Would you like a biscuit?"

"That would be wonderful," replied Marta with a warm smile, thinking not only was he handsome, but thoughtful too! Mash stopped stirring the embers for a second and returned her gaze in a friendly way.

"OUCHHH, what the . . . !" screamed Smidge. "I am on fire! Ouchhhhh!"

One of the sparks had landed in Smidge's fur, and smoke was streaming from his leg as he ran around the fire. The two squirrels broke off their mutual perusal, and Mash chased after Smidge.

"Stop running and let me smother the flame with a blanket!"

Pete, still in some sort of dream, muttered grumpily, "Don't put the fire out, I am cold. Fan the flame."

Smidge, yelling louder, glared at Pete. "Some friend you are!" He jumped up and down, smacking his leg furiously with his paws.

Using Pete's belly as a jumping platform, Mash leapt across the fire and tackled Smidge.

"Oh my goodness, I ate too much, my stomach hurts," moaned Pete, rolling over and falling back to sleep.

Rolling Smidge vigorously in the dirt, Mash quickly extinguished the flames.

From under the blankets, Marta watched the frantic action until she could no longer contain her laughter.

"What's she laughing at? I am on fire!"

"Not now, you goof. You're all right. The fire's out," sputtered Mash breathlessly.

"Oh no, the fire's out," mumbled Pete. "But I am cold."

"Hey, you didn't have to hit me so hard. You hurt my leg!" complained Smidge.

"Then go jump in the stream and cool it down," suggested Mash. "You *are* an otter."

"Yeah, go jump in the stream," yelled Pete, who then quickly resumed his snorting snore.

"Everyone stop!" implored Marta with tears of laughter rolling down her face.

Clutching her sides with laughter reminded her of the wound in her brother's side, and Marta suddenly awoke out of the fog she had been in. She shook her head to clear it. Hazy memories started to rush into her mind, and she felt a powerful tide of anxiety and fear wash over her. Seeing the sudden change of expression on her beautiful face, Mash rushed closer.

"What's the matter? You look sick!"

"I am not sure, but I think I lost something really important."

ço

The sleep was deep and heavy. His dreams were filled with pain and sword fighting and more pain. The cold awakened him. His eyes opened and slowly he became aware of his surroundings. Struggling to make sense of the situation in which he found himself, he lay on the cold stony path for some time, too weak to do anything but let the darkness of night envelop him.

Shivering, Alex sensed something on his paw and arm. A smooth, cool sensation . . . moving . . . up toward his neck. His paws felt heavy as he tried to reach up to—yuck, the hideous sensation started moving across his face. His paws gained strength as the serpent hissed in his ear. Able to half raise himself, he tossed the three-foot milk snake into the woods. Its green iridescence quickly blended into the night as it slithered away.

The sudden movements had sent pain shooting across Alex's belly, but at least he was awake, which he hadn't been for— well, he didn't know for how long. Lying back down, he tried to sort through his jumbled thoughts.

Where was Marta? Something terrible must have happened for her to leave him alone. He was terrified . . . of the dark, of all the strange noises . . . but he realized he had to try to move. Painfully working out the stiffness in his muscles caused from lying motionless for so long, he eventually rose to his paws.

Turning slowly, he couldn't decide which direction to take along the path. Finally, knowing that he had to find warmth, food and some help, he forced himself to walk. Staggering and pausing frequently, he kept one paw pressed against his bandaged wound, trying to stop the flow of warm, sticky blood.

ତ

The large, white rabbit sat squarely on his haunches near a low, burning fire, rapidly turning a large turnip in his paws. As the vegetable spun, the buck took large bites out of it with his long incisors. Juice and pieces of vegetable flew outward, some landing in the fire with a sizzle and pop.

The ravenous diner seemed oblivious to everything around him. His eyes closed and opened in a gentle rhythm of contentment, and soon the turnip disappeared. After licking his paws, he grunted and rummaged in a huge sack near his feet. Triumphant, he pulled out another enormous turnip. Spinning it in his powerful paws, he began to sing:

Was there ever a turnip
That I didn't like?
Was there ever any food
That I wouldn't bite?
If you don't think
That this is right,
Go take a hike!

A small, blackened pot on the fire began to boil and the long-eared rabbit removed it from the flame and poured the hot liquid into a wooden cup filled with green leaves. "Gotty to have me tea, tea, tea!"

Affecting a different voice, he began interviewing himself. "And why is that?"

Returning to his normal voice, he replied, "It is the drink of royalty!"

The interviewer asked, "But surely you are not a king?"

"No, not a king. But, I most certainly am royalty. I am a duke. I have just temporarily misplaced my dukedom."

"How can one do that? I think you are a lowly turnip thief and an impostor!"

"Go take a hike!" the rabbit retorted. Then he broke into a hearty laugh that ended in a fit of coughing. "Oh my, I must stop smoking my tea leaves!"

He was still coughing and laughing when he heard a rustling in the bushes. With a speed and agility unexpected from such a large, rotund beast, he dove over the fire, rolled once on his shoulder and whisked a large sword from its sheath on his waist. Standing taut with anticipation, he slowly searched the surrounding bushes. His breath came hard, highlighted by the firelight that filled the misty air. With one rear paw, he stretched back and deftly overturned the remainder of the pot of water to douse the fire. Now his eyes could adjust to the darkness, and his silhouette against the flames was eliminated.

Adjusting the grip on his sword and widening his stance in anticipation of an attack, he moved slowly toward the source of the noise. The bushes swayed from side to side and then parted abruptly as a squirrel staggered forward with a glazed look in its eyes. Detecting no threat from the beast, the rabbit lowered his sword. As he approached, he could see a bandage surrounded by a dark blotch of blood covering the squirrel's stomach. Unexpectedly, the intruder lurched and began to fall. Rushing forward and catching the beast with his free arm, the rabbit lowered the wounded squirrel to the ground. Always the wary warrior, he scanned the edge of the forest to ensure this was not a trick and that there were no more attackers. Determining there was no further threat, he dragged the limp body toward his campfire.

Once he had re-sheathed his sword and placed some dry leaves on the remaining hot coals to restart the fire, the rabbit began tending to the wounded squirrel. He carefully assessed the victim, stopping only to add wood to the flames to get a good blaze going. The creature had turned pale, and his pulse beat weakly. He noted the bandage and herbal ointment that had been applied. There were no wounds other than the one in the belly, probably inflicted by a knife. In these forests, it was most likely from a rat's filthy blade.

But if some beast had already cared for this squirrel, why was he wandering around alone and delirious in the forest? Were the attackers close by, and would they be paying a visit to his camp? He knew the fire might attract them, but he had no choice. This poor beast needed warmth. No worries. If the scoundrels did pay a visit, he would gladly settle the score. He covered the mysterious visitor with his blanket before wrapping himself in his own well-worn, green tartan cloak. Wearily, he leaned against a log, placed his sword by his side and fell into an uneasy sleep.

The usual dream came over him. Black… black rats, hundreds of them, standing row upon row, spear butts pounding on the earth in unison, causing the ground to shudder, constantly advancing. His paw reached for his sword.

Waking with a start, his heart pounding, he blinked his eyes clear. There was no danger, only the sounds of the forest at night. He settled back and resigned himself to another long night spent without sleep.

7

THE BATTLE OF MUDDY MOSS

Muddy Moss Moor

Eager to fill his larders ever fuller for the winter, the crazed King Magnath sent his troops out frequently to prey on farmers, but not even Aswar had anticipated that he'd be dispatched the morning following the feast. He and his weary troops had risen before dawn and marched eastward double-time, throughout the day and night, to reach the edge of the Lowlands by the following morning. The beasts below had not noticed a pair of scouts from Magnath camping in the hills, spying. Once preparations for the harvest market had become evident, one of the rats had run the long journey to the castle in just one day to alert the king. Now the raiders rested in the hills, awaiting their orders.

As Aswar rubbed sleep from his eyes, the glimmer of the early morning light danced along his blade and made the instrument of death seem much prettier than it deserved to be. Aswar shifted his position to gain some comfort as he surveyed the scene below.

The inhabitants of Muddy Moss were going about the business of preparing for another hectic day of trading. Farmers with carts filled with turnips, sweet ruby beets, corn and sheaves of wheat were moving toward the bargaining area. This circular marketplace was laid with wooden planks to prevent the heavily burdened carts from sinking into the mud if it should rain. In the centre of the circle was a large, raised wooden platform, where farmers were unloading samples of their produce and potential traders were inspecting it. In the centre of the platform were enormous rectangular tables, stacked high with blankets, pots and pans, knives, wooden tables, chairs and many other wares manufactured by the villagers. The display tables had been crafted from heavy oak logs to support this wealth of goods.

For generations, these Woodlanders had flourished in this lush land that lay between the forest and the sea. The forest provided an abundance of building materials for the villagers, and the fertile soil of the lowlands produced ample crops. The surrounding woods had also provided protection from the army of Magnath. Still, the villagers had taken precautions. Although the elaborate trading area was large, the mice merchants could quickly move the camp into clever hiding places in the woods if a threat should arise.

Aswar continued to observe the scene, knowing his king would be very pleased. Even if they captured only half the enormous amount of food on display, the castle stores would be full. In addition, he was certain to find some item of beauty that would catch the king's greedy eye and serve as a trophy of the conquest. The usual orders had been given for the battle that day: pillage, but leave as many villagers and farmers alive as possible so that they could be robbed again the following harvest. The command to spare lives gave him some comfort as he turned his gaze from the peaceful scene of friendly commerce to the mass of black-armoured rats behind him, eager to attack. He re-sheathed his weapon and waited for more carts to arrive, filled with supplies destined for the king's larder.

❧

Tall and strong for a Woodlander mouse, Ting was a barter agent who made sure the rules of fairness applied to all the transactions among the farmers, the fisher otters and the forest folk. He loved the sounds and smells of these glorious fall days when the trading circle filled with voices, the aromas of fresh-baked breads and the scents of onions, leeks, peppers and tomatoes. That evening would see the first of several feasts and dances celebrating the bountiful harvest.

But these market days were also the most dangerous of the year. The Woodlanders were most vulnerable to attack when they emerged from the forest to conduct business.

Ting's calm manner was welcomed by each of the traders. He was not only a barter agent, but also one of the leaders of the Woodland Militia, and on his belt he carried a small, curved dagger with a lethal cutting edge. As he watched the carts being unloaded, he frequently surveyed the hills and woods around the bustling camp. It had been some time since they had unwelcome visitors, but he and the other militia members always kept an uneasy watch.

Woodlanders, because they were frequently moving about, had never developed the skill of forging steel to make swords and armour. They had traded with a few travelling scoundrels to obtain some fighting hardware, such as his dagger, but bows and arrows were their main defence. At every harvest, a wide variety of local creatures volunteered to help protect their fellow Woodlanders and farmers. The Woodland Militia had guards posted in the surrounding trees with slings and arrows at the ready. Their squirrel leader was the colourful One Eye One Shot.

He approached Ting on his way to the forest. "Well, friend, I think I'll be heading up to the trees now. I hope this glorious sunny day will be filled with peace and prosperity for all." The squirrel leader patted Ting on the shoulder.

"Yes, it should be a very successful day. A reason to celebrate well into the late hours tonight," answered Ting as he watched his ally depart, glad to have such a strong, powerful squirrel on their side. One Eye One Shot, or One Eye as he was most often called, told everyone who would listen about how he had lost his eye battling a weasel. In reality, as a youngster running around a campfire, he had disregarded his parents' warning and had fallen while carrying a burning stick. Worried that he would not be allowed to be a soldier with only one eye, he had practised archery to become so proficient that he was nicknamed One Eye One Shot.

ల

Sweat began to fill Aswar's armour as the sun continued its ascent in the morning sky. His troops were getting restless, and if they didn't attack soon, detection was inevitable. Adjusting his black helmet and drawing his sword, he nodded his head to the runners beside him. They scurried off to ready the co-commanders for battle. Within moments, a squad of lance rats silently moved down a dry streamed on the right flank to a hiding position in the woods just past the camp. Simultaneously, on the left flank, archers crept downhill behind a knoll with instructions not to fire until ordered. With his flanks covered, Aswar raised his sword and motioned forward.

Ting's eyes immediately saw the glint of sun on steel, but it took a moment for him to overcome his panic and sound the alarm. "We're under attack! Run for cover!"

Bedlam ensued, with elders and children hiding under carts and the Woodland Militia running to fetch slings and bows. Ting was amazed to see the quiet hillside transformed into a volcanic eruption as streams of black rats flowed toward them. He would have almost preferred deadly hot lava to the blood-curdling battle cry of the rats!

Ting recovered his senses and ran to organize the ranks of archers. The well-trained militia had drilled for many hours and were already forming lines, preparing to fire, but fear and anxiety were causing some to become confused.

Ting drew a line in the dirt with his blade. "First line, here. Second line, two paces back of them, and third line, two paces behind them."

Hastily, the stragglers joined the tight rows and loaded their arrows. Ting turned to see the enemy already within range.

"First row, up. Fire! Down. Second row, up. Fire! Down. Third row, up. Fire!" As he repeated himself over and over, the arrows flew off the taut strings toward the charging horde.

Aswar ran behind his troops, surprised to see such an organized defence. Arrows were hailing down with relentless regularity. Two charging rats fell awkwardly as arrows struck their uncovered lower legs, and another was felled instantly with an arrow through the neck. The fast-moving soldiers behind stumbled over their fallen comrades. Rising quickly,

they continued onward, yelling fiercely. Ting was worried. He could see their arrows were having little effect. Where were One Eye and the squirrels? Suddenly, an idea struck him as he looked around the camp and saw an open fire.

"Third row, over here. Light your arrows! First and second row, keep firing!" The rats leading the advance could see some of the archers running. Sensing victory, they charged harder.

Ting could see things were about to get worse very quickly. He commanded the archers not to return to their ranks but to quickly fire burning arrows at the dry autumn grass in front of the advancing army. Without material wrapped around the

arrow to burn, the wood shaft itself
had to carry the flame.

Most of the arrows landed with
their flame extinguished. Others flew
off course as their feathers burned and
their balance was lost.

Realizing his plan was not working,
Ting ordered retreat, but as his archers
began to disperse, he heard horrific
screams from the direction of the
rats. One of the arrows must

have stayed lit long enough to ignite the dry grass in a flash into a wall of flames.

Fanned by the breeze, the roaring flames swept toward the rat army. One Eye One Shot eagerly watched the dramatic events unfold below. He had waited his whole life to be a warrior, and this was his chance! He had planned his strategy, but sticking to it was difficult. Seeing how ineffectual the mice's arrows had been, One Eye had decided to wait for the vermin to come closer.

The squirrels' arrows were larger and more likely to penetrate thick armour, but only at close range. As they approached, the rats would also be in sling-stone range. With a pounding heart and sweaty paws, he waited to order the attack. His spirits soared when Ting's fiery assault stopped the rats in their tracks, but he knew the grass fire would quickly die out from lack of fuel. Seizing the moment, he raised his bow. Immediately, the band brought arrows to bows and stones to slings. The rats were in range!

"Fire!" One Eye yelled fiercely, releasing his own arrow with a twang of the string. Twenty arrows and twenty stones arched through the air toward the unsuspecting black rats. One Eye's squirrel band had almost reloaded when the thudding sound of the projectiles hitting their targets carried back to the treetops. Twelve rats fell dead instantly, their armour pierced by the sturdy squirrel arrows, and another four were struck dead by stone blows to the head. Countless others were wounded or dazed. Confusion set in as the rats searched for the source of the unexpected attack.

Ting, seeing the rats' advance stopped by the squirrels' ferocious volley, called his archers back into formation. Once the first volley of arrows took flight, he turned his attention momentarily to the chaos in the trading circle around him.

"Get those carts into the woods!" he commanded. Despite his order, many of the mice tried to gather up more food into their baskets and carts. Frustrated, Ting screamed, "Leave it! Run, you fools. It will be of no use if you are dead! Now go!"

Thick, black smoke blew toward Aswar and the waiting troops, causing the commander's eyes to water, but he had seen enough. This was not going according to plan. What should have been a simple task of scaring away the merchants and farmers had become a pitched battle. Disappointed, Aswar beckoned his runners, Fast Paws and Wing. He gave the order for the lance rodents on the right flank to move forward from their hiding spot in the woods to cut off the stream of fleeing carts. Fast Paws ran off with the message, while Wing received the command for the archers on the left to advance to the next knoll and destroy the mouse archers.

One Eye One Shot was delighted at the success of his first broadside, but now the rats were spreading out and reforming, preparing to renew the attack. Should his band stay aloft in the trees or join the fray below? The grass fire burned rapidly from the main battle area toward a grove of tall maples on the flank, and as it cleared the tall grass and bushes in its path, a frightening sight emerged behind its billowing smoke. Crouching amongst the trees was an entire squad of rats armed with wicked-looking lances. If they outflanked the unarmed beasts fleeing with the harvest, all would be lost. The lance rats had to be dealt with immediately, but they were out of range. He would have to take the fight to them! Upon his command, the squirrels jumped across the branches to the edge of the forest and down into the charred remains of the grassland.

Fast Paws choked on the smoke as he ran toward the lance squad. He had no armour so he could keep up his speed. His only weapon was a small curved knife strapped to his back. Upon descending the hill, he found it difficult to stay oriented in the smoky haze.

Without warning, Fast Paws found himself in the midst of a hard-running pack of squirrels. The impact was thunderous as he collided with one, then two of the squirrels, and all three beasts fell to the ground. Although stunned, he whipped out his blade and immediately brought it down on the squirrel lying beside him, thus eliminating half of the immediate danger. It took a moment in the confusion to locate the other squirrel and dispatch him before he fully regained his senses. Then Fast Paws hesitated, trying to find his bearings—it was the last thing he did before One Eye's arrow pierced his heart. Fast Paws' message to the lance rats would not be delivered.

In the urgency of battle, One Eye had no time to mourn the first loss of life under his command. Two of his squirrels were dead, but he rallied his troops onward toward the rat lance squad.

Ting encouraged his archers to stand their ground as the rats' lethal hailstorm of arrows arrived. Half of the first row of his archers went down, and a few from the other rows as well. The rat archers had found a knoll untouched by the flames on which to mount an attack. Outflanked, and knowing what was coming, Ting had no option but to retreat with the remainder of the troops.

They were close to escaping into the woods when the rats found their range and a round of arrows took down eight more Woodlanders. Ting lurched forward, stumbling as his right leg went numb and gave out. Then the searing pain started, and he fell awkwardly, crashing headlong into a tree with an arrow deep in his thigh. The remaining fighters retreated into the forest as Ting lay motionless, oblivious to the advancing rats.

જી

One Eye One Shot knew the enemy lance beasts were in the smoke up ahead but could not understand why they were not attacking. Not wondering for long, he dispersed his troops along a ditch filled with dogwood and hackberry bushes and spared by the fire. After letting loose with a volley of arrows and sling-stones, the squirrels ducked into the ditch so as not to give away their new position.

The leader of the rat lancers was furious. With no orders, they were waiting, stomping out the advancing flames, roasting like chestnuts in their armour. Now arrows were landing in their midst from who knows where. Action was what his rat warriors wanted, and action was what they would get!

"Lances up! Attack!" he commanded.

One Eye had timed the moment perfectly for his next broadside. The captain and many of his lance rats lost their lives with the second deadly rain of arrows and stones. The remaining rats ran every which way in a panic as they deserted the battle.

Savouring his first victory of war, One Eye One Shot's celebration was short-lived as the smoke cleared and he saw that the rest of the battle had been lost.

Ting and his troops were nowhere to be seen, and rats were rushing around the trading circle, pillaging the harvest left behind. One Eye summoned his band, and they returned to the forest to protect the survivors, who were fleeing with anything they could carry.

જી

Aswar stood in the middle of the trading circle surveying the meagre stash of loot. Magnath would not be pleased at all. He had lost many fighters, some to death and many to desertion. He sensed some of the captains were questioning his leadership. Spying a colourful carpet, woven from rushes and dyed with root pigments, he scooped it up. He hoped that it would serve as an offering to quell his king's anger. It was going to be a long march home indeed.

8

HEALING PAWS

North of Muddy Moss Moor

Ting awoke to find himself being pulled, bumping and banging, through the forest by some creature with a firm grasp on his neck fur. The pain in his leg burned and every brush with a tree or knock on a log felt like a knife twisting deep inside it. He could see an arrow protruding from his right thigh, but of more immediate concern was the difficulty he was having breathing. As his captor dragged him, the skin around his neck had been drawn up tight, choking him. The gurgling sounds from his throat were the only noises he could make, and his wiggling did nothing to alert his captor to his plight.

Using all his strength, he turned onto his left side, away from his injured leg and grabbed an ash sapling. He thought his head might be pulled off his shoulders as his captor pulled even harder to counter the resistance. He felt faint as a clump of his fur painfully tore away. An angry yelp exploded from his abductor as the sudden release of his captive caused him to crash forward. His powerful momentum carried him through the bushes into a shallow ditch filled with stagnant water and rotting leaves.

"You ungrateful little mouse!" cursed the mud-covered beast as he wiped grunge from his mouth and nose. "Another arrow should finish you off," he threatened, clutching his bow so tightly his paws shook.

The wounded Woodlander replied, "It wouldn't be good sport not to give me a chance to defend myself." He felt along his belt for his dagger.

"Well, you better start running. I'll give you the count of three," roared the mud figure.

"I can't run. So knives it is!" Ting retorted, pulling out his dagger.

"Sorry, too much work!" replied the warrior, raising his bow with an arrow ready. "Besides, you have a good chance since I only got one good eye and it's filled with mud." He started to chuckle.

"One Eye One Shot! It's you under all that mud!"

"Yeah, 'tis me. Frayed nerves. Sorry I lost my temper. How is your leg, Ting?"

"I think if you dragged me into any more trees, you would have pushed the arrow through the other side."

"Well, if you hadn't grabbed that tree and landed me in here, I could have finished the job."

They both started to laugh as the tension of the battle began to lift from their minds and they realized they were well away from danger. As the rats had overrun the Woodlanders' defences, the terrified beasts had run every which way in panicked retreat. One Eye and his remaining squirrel warriors had run back to the woods to protect the withdrawal. Along the way, they had snatched as many of the wounded as they could and dragged them into the woods, away from the savagery of the marauding rats.

Looking back toward the camp, One Eye had spotted Ting at the edge of the woods. Telling the rest of his band to carry on, he had crept back slowly, without being detected by the rats, and grabbed his friend. Not wanting to be caught, One Eye had turned and run as fast as he could, never looking back to see if the Woodlander he pulled was alive or dead.

One Eye rose, stripped some leaves off a dogwood bush and wiped his face and paws clean with them. Kneeling at Ting's side, he gently examined the wound. "It's nasty, Ting. I'll cut the arrow shaft shorter so it doesn't get in the way. We'd better get to a healer fast. There is one across the river to the north." Shouldering his friend, he started walking swiftly north toward the river. "Don't you worry, she is a good healer."

But there was no response, as the wounded Woodlander had passed out from the pain.

Rough Wood Forest

Sopping wet and exhausted from crossing the Big Chute River while holding Ting out of the frigid water, One Eye paused to catch his breath. With water still dripping into his eyes, he surveyed the high wall of stone close to the bank. The stones were dark with moss and had been carefully arranged to blend in with the side of the riverbank. Covered with thorn bushes, the wall was a formidable barrier, only penetrable through a door of randomly arranged sticks that cleverly camouflaged the opening.

A soft moan escaped his friend's mouth when One Eye carefully laid him down. Just as he reached for the door latch, a voice coming from the bushes to the left caused him to jump with surprise.

"State your bizz-in-ness," uttered a low baritone voice with a slight French accent.

"Pierre, it's me, One Eye One Shot, with a wounded friend. Let us in quickly, he's near death!"

"Turn and let me see your faaace."

One Eye impatiently turned toward the unseen inquisitor.

"Ahh, indeed, eh one-eye squi'rrle. You may enter and let me help you wid your frriend." A large beaver with enormous yellow teeth emerged from the bushes, carrying a wooden spear gnawed perfectly into a lethal-looking point.

The two beasts picked up the limp form of Ting and carried him through the gate toward a ramshackle wooden hut. They were greeted at the hut's doorway by a plump beaver with flowers braided into the longer hairs behind her ears and a white apron around her waist, decorated with colourful embroidery. Her accent was much thicker than her husband's.

"Mon Dieu, whut dooo wee 'ave ici?"

"My friend is wounded, Giselle. He needs your healing."

"Entrez, tout de suite! Pierre, more wood on de firre." With deft paws, Giselle quickly removed the arrow and tended the wound. When she was done, a thick bandage bound the injury tightly. "He will be okay doekay, your ami, mais not for some time."

Pierre found an enormous beaver blanket to warm the shivering squirrel. The coarse blanket was so big that One Eye had to wrap the lower part around himself three times so he wouldn't trip.

Pierre, now comfortably sitting in a chair on the other side of the fire, had questions.

"Well, One Eye, 'ow did this 'appen?"

With a mug of hot cider and a scone, One Eye settled in to relate the events of the battle.

⁕

Delirious, Ting moaned softly, sometimes reaching into the air with his paws as if he were shooting arrows.

One Eye paused momentarily to look at his friend with a worried expression on his face and then continued telling Pierre the details of the horrible battle. He was reassured to see Giselle wiping Ting's sweat-covered forehead with moss, soaked in cool water. The injured warrior, comforted by his nurse, lowered his arms and fell into a deep sleep.

"Those black rats showed no mercy, stripping the place bare. It was a devastating sight to see so many killed. My heart will not rest until I have revenge!" said the angry squirrel.

"Reeevenge is a dangerrrous t'ing, mon ami. It will only lead to more pain and death. It is best you move on and find a safer 'ome," cautioned Pierre softly, stroking his grey whiskers.

"I would if I thought that was possible, but those rats are raiding farther and farther to satisfy their greed! They will always come back! No place is safe!"

"Where do these rrrrats come from?"

"There is a fortress west of here, near the Slave Trader's Sea, that is ruled by a tyrant named Magnath. He constantly seeks more and more. He has so many soldiers that he has trouble feeding them all, unless he pillages farther and farther away from his castle. No one will be safe, not even the Farlanders of the Rough Wood Forest."

Pierre tapped the unburned leaves from his large, ornately carved pipe and contemplated what this news meant to him and the French Farlanders. They had been isolated for so long from other beasts and the troubles they caused, they had not worried about conflict. Yes, he had heard of Magnath. His ancestors had travelled west from the Lake Regions of the Eastern Territory many seasons ago to be pioneers in this rich land of streams and forests, but the rats had halted their westward progress. Although the Farlanders created a strong army to protect themselves, they chose to retreat far from Magnath.

One season at Big Chute River, Pierre and his family had met One Eye's father, a brave squirrel who had explored the Rough Wood Forest farther than any other beast. Over the seasons, Giselle had traded her healing skills for fresh nuts and other goods the squirrel had brought. The two families had become good friends, and after his father had died, One Eye had often visited the wise old beavers for advice.

The Farlanders living in the Rough Wood Forest were peace-loving farmers and forest dwellers, spread out over a vast territory stretching north and east from Big Chute River. One Eye was right. What would stop the rats from attacking? Their small isolated villages would be easy targets for the rat army. Despite each community training a volunteer fighting force, the Farlanders had never developed a coordinated defence system. In fact, the only time they really spoke to each other was once each season at the council meeting held at the largest village, Castorville. Representatives from every region met to discuss news and trade their goods. Pierre himself was due to leave in a couple of days for the fall meeting, a day's travel along two rivers.

"I think you 'ave a good point, mon ami. I will carry your news to the council meeting. We must prepare ourselves against this evil."

"No, Pierre, your people must do more than that!"

"What do you mean?"

"Let me explain," said One Eye as he moved his chair closer to the big beaver. Before he spoke, he glanced again at his wounded comrade to reassure himself he was alive. What he could see were the gently breathing movements of Ting's chest.

The Valley of Stone

Gerr was leading a search party of twenty otter and squirrel volunteers. Pete's father, Ralph, had been worried he would slow the team and had volunteered to stay with Silk to maintain a vigil in case the wandering young ones came home. Too old for such trips, Harnath, the otter leader, had agreed to let Gerr lead the search party.

The search party's first stop was the Valley of Stone to see if the two young ones had paid Mash and Dash a visit. They made camp near the huge oak tree, home of Grunch and Misty. Grunch, looking tired and dirty, explained after some hurried greetings that he also had been out searching, because Mash was missing too. He apologized profusely that he had not personally made sure the young ones had returned to Manorwood, and promised to join the search party the next morning.

9

FRIENDS AND FANGS

Tullymug Woods

Spit had slept poorly at the side of the trail. Resuming his journey before dawn, he shifted the heavy pack of wares on his back and trudged along the path. He was not singing anymore, for he was deep in thought. He struggled to get Marta and her brother out of his mind. He couldn't believe his feelings—he actually liked that Marta. Her bravery and honesty had melted some of his natural cynicism. It had been a little harder to get to know Alex, since he had been unconscious, but he was feeling an emotion he was not accustomed to: guilt. Would he want to be left defenceless in the middle of a forest? He answered his own question by turning on his heels and running back along the path toward the place where he'd left the injured squirrel.

Turning at a bend in the path, he could not believe his eyes. The blanket lay crumpled in the pathway, but Alex was gone! Glad that the lad was still alive, and at the same time frustrated that he had lost him, he scanned the area for clues. Looking on each side of the path, he studied the bushes for evidence that they had been disturbed. A few broken twigs and some scuffed up leaves seemed to indicate a beast had headed across the path to the north. Had Alex awakened or had he been abducted? The forest looked dark and thick and scary, and was certainly not a place Spit normally would ever think of entering. Not knowing what to do, he started to retrace his steps, but when he rounded the first bend his pace slowed with indecision. Resting his back against a large cedar tree, he slid slowly to the ground and covered his eyes with his paws. A long moan escaped from his lips, ending with a snort and an unusually large spit.

"Darn sinuses!"

☙

After quickly introducing his friends, Mash encouraged Marta to tell them what important thing she had lost. She felt sick to her stomach as she urgently related the story about her wounded brother and their confrontation with the rats.

"Well, that certainly was something important you misplaced! Sometimes I wish I could lose my brother!" exclaimed Mash.

"Be careful what you wish for," cautioned Pete.

"How would you know, Pete? You don't have a brother," joked Mash unknowingly.

"There you go, I guess my wish came true," murmured Pete.

"We must find Alex at once!" urged Marta, wiping hot tears from her eyes.

"Let's start looking upstream," commanded Mash, picking up his spear and throwing his gear into his pack. "The sun is starting to rise. Let's go!"

The group spread out and picked their way through thick underbrush. Marta called out her brother's name every few minutes. Their progress was slow, and Mash became frustrated.

"I am going up into the trees to look around. I can travel faster that way." He scurried up an enormous basswood with limbs stretching out like highways. With arching jumps, Mash expertly travelled through the tree canopy, and in a minute, spotted a crumpled blanket on the forest path and directed the others toward it.

Marta, Smidge and Pete crashed through the bushes onto the path as Mash descended swiftly along a half fallen branch. As they regrouped, they heard a loud snort followed by a big . . .

"Spit!" cried Marta, turning and running frantically away from them.

"What the heck! Where is she going?" exclaimed Smidge.

"Guys, she seems nice enough, but I think she may have mental health issues," panted Pete.

The companions turned and followed the excited squirrel, with Mash in the lead and Pete struggling to keep up. As they rounded a bend, they skidded to a stop and witnessed Marta chasing a mouse with a broken stick.

"You horrible creature, what do you mean you don't know where he is? You little, lying rodent . . . you spit factory . . . you scumball!"

The fearful mouse, who had not been able to grab his sword in time, stumbled to the ground and covered his head with his arms, pulling his cloak over his face.

"How could you lose my brother?" Marta ranted at the cowering beast.

Mash rushed forward and held Marta's arm just as she was about to smash the helpless mouse into extinction. "He will

be no good to us dead, Marta. Let him explain. Perhaps we can get an idea of where Alex is."

Hearing her companions subdue Marta, the huckster regained some of his confidence. "Let me explain, will ya!"

Marta relaxed her arm and stopped fighting against Mash's firm grip. But just as he let go, she delivered one quick blow to the mouse's bottom.

"Ouch! No fair. What'd you do that for?"

"Make it quick or I let her finish the job," Mash said with an angry look in his eyes.

"He was just lying on the blanket unconscious-like, and I just went . . . um . . . a short way . . . ah . . . down the path to . . . er . . . scout things out. When I got back, he was gone."

"You left him, and some beast or something has taken him. You heartless cheese-head!" sobbed Marta.

"Look, I noticed some leaves had been moved over there, and I think he went that way into the forest. I was just planning my search when you attacked me, you ungrateful nutcracker," retorted Spit with boldness returning to his voice.

"Stop it, you two! He's right. It looks like some beast has gone this way," yelled Smidge, as he examined the side of the path near the blanket.

"Who is this creature, Marta?" demanded Mash, indicating the dirty-looking mouse.

Spit rose to his paws quickly, filth billowing from his clothes as he brushed himself off. Sputtering in the dust cloud, the stubby mouse cleared his throat loudly. "Allow me to introduce myself. I am Spit. I travel far and wide, selling the finest goods the world can provide." After this immodest proclamation, he launched one of his spitballs into the forest.

"Yuck, how appropriate," remarked Pete.

"A painful sinus condition, you know. Not my fault. Anyway, I travel these lands selling fine merchandise to rich and poor."

"I am sure they are all poorer after meeting you," said Mash under his breath. Then he spoke up. "So you know this area well, do you?"

"Like the back of me mother's paw, I do."

"Which I am sure you saw a lot of as she tried to smack some sense into you. Well, I suppose you can help. Stop talking, gather up your wares, and let's find Marta's brother." Mash gave the mouse a shove toward the area of the woods that Smidge was exploring.

Spit cast a wary glance around the group. Marta's eyes were still angry, Smidge and Mash looked tough and all business, but Pete didn't look particularly interested in anything but a long rest. With his sense of guilt wearing thin, Spit had no interest in anything that might take him too far from his travels. There was just too much money to make!

Gathering up his wares, Spit tried to placate Marta and her friends. "Look, I don't know anything other than the paths. I never go into the forest, so I won't be of any use. I'd just slow you down with my crippled leg. I think I'll be on my way." The mouse headed in the other direction, limping badly.

"What crippled leg? You move just fine when you want to!" said Marta in an exasperated tone.

"It's when the weather changes. Oh no, you wouldn't want me around, that's for sure." To ensure his quick and safe departure, he added, "Anyway, Marta, I have been thinking that I didn't make a fair deal with you, and I would like to return your sword."

Reaching into his largest pack, he withdrew the impressive weapon and unwrapped it from the oily cloth he had used to protect it from rust. When the surprised Marta took it into her paw, the mouse turned and bolted down the path, calling over his shoulder, "Good luck, bye!"

"The sword you stole, you mean!" screamed Marta, pursuing the mouse merchant.

Mash shot out his arm and placed it on her shoulder to stop her. "I think it's best that he goes. We'll be fine. Let's go find Alex."

They easily followed the trail of disturbed leaves and broken twigs Smidge had found. Whoever had journeyed this way had made no effort to hide his passage. Mash paused for a moment every once in a while and flicked away rusty, red-stained leaves with the tip of his sword. There was no sense upsetting Marta by letting her see the blood, but it made him confident they were on the correct trail.

Rounding a large rock, Mash stopped. "I smell smoke!"

Instinctively, they dropped to the ground for cover and searched the forest with their eyes and keen sense of smell.

"Over that way," whispered Smidge as he crawled up beside Mash and indicated a hollow beyond a group of large white pine trees.

Pete rose to his foot paws, his nose twitching in anticipation. "Where there is smoke, there is fire, and where there is fire, some beast is making breakfast."

"Shut up and get down, you fool!" ordered Mash.

Marta, eager to find her brother, crept quickly toward the smoky smell, with Smidge in pursuit.

"Slow down. Be careful, Marta."

The three friends scurried along the forest floor after Marta. Pulling her into cover behind a rotting log, they peeked at a large rabbit tending a fire. Even from a distance, they could see the power in his shoulders and muscular arms as he moved a burning log with a very big sword.

None of this deterred Marta from jumping over the log and dashing forward as she sighted the prone form of Alex by the fire. "Alex, Alex, are you alright?"

For his size, the rabbit was unnervingly quick. He was in a fighting posture with his sword thrust forward, on the ready, before Marta had yelled Alex's name for the second time. "Stop right there and put your paws in the air."

Marta did not have ears for the warning and remained totally focused on reaching Alex.

Mash knew a disaster in the making when he saw one and jumped out of the forest with an arrow taut on his bowstring. "Stand aside. She means no harm."

The rabbit looked from the obviously distraught maiden rushing toward him to the young squirrel who had a very fierce look in his eyes. He looked strong for his age and had a taut bow, loaded with a hefty arrow aimed at the rabbit's heart. Slowly, the rabbit lowered his sword and re-sheathed it. "Be careful, miss, he is badly wounded."

"I know,' she sobbed, her head on Alex's chest. "He's my brother."

Rough Wood Forest

At first light, Pierre awakened One Eye from a heavy sleep and led him to the riverbank. The beaver slid into the dark water and called for One Eye to jump on his back.

"Whoa! You didn't tell me about this! This is crazy!" yelled One Eye as he steadied himself near the broad head of the half-submerged beaver.

"How else are we going to get down de riverrr? Trust me, I am a goooood driver!" replied Pierre as he pushed away from the shore into the current. "Hooold tight."

"Hold onto what? There is nothing to grab onto back here."

"Certainement, 'der ees so. Try grabbing a few of de longer, thicker hairs on my shoulders."

They had barely moved any distance down the river when a roaring sound reached One Eye's keen ears. With alarm in his voice, the squirrel screamed, "What's that noise?"

Just then the river took a turn and the current sped up. Ahead, rapids surged around huge boulders like a horizontal waterfall.

"You didn't tell me about rapids!"

"Oui. Now you see why, if you don't hold on, you will die . . . certainement," replied the beaver calmly.

Just in time, as the first wave of foaming water thrust over the beaver's back, the terrified passenger desperately grabbed a lifeline of long shoulder hairs. When the next swirl of current pushed the beaver's entire body below the surface, One Eye's firm grasp prevented him from being swept away. He had no time to take a breath before they were submerged again. When the squirrel surfaced, he was gasping, spitting water from his mouth. Pulling himself to his knees above the heaving water, he sputtered, "I might die even if I do hold on!"

"Certainement, but we are almost through."

"Stop with the 'certainement' stuff . . . Whoa, look out!"

The squirrel barely had time to get his arm up to protect his head as the boiling water whipped them under a willow branch extending over the riverbank. One Eye's cry of surprise could barely be heard above the din as he was picked up off the beaver's shoulders and suspended above the current with his paw firmly wedged in a fork of the tree branch.

"Pierre! Pierre! Help!" he cried. But his voice was lost in the noise as the beaver navigated through the rocks and whitewater. The soaking wet squirrel watched until Pierre disappeared out of sight. "Well, mon ami, you certainement are in trouble now," One Eye muttered under his breath, imitating the beaver's accent.

His right shoulder felt like it was being pulled out of its socket, as his entire weight swung back and forth, hanging by one arm. His foot paws skimmed the surface of the frothing river. No matter how he stretched, he couldn't reach the branch with his other paw. One Eye continued to ponder his fate, held prisoner by the willow branch over the churning water. A chill ran down his spine when he faced the shore. A snake—a water moccasin—was slithering through the water directly toward his paws. If this didn't motivate him to reach his knife, nothing would!

Ignoring the pain in his trapped paw as he twisted, he reached across his body and grabbed the knife with his other paw. He watched anxiously as the deadly serpent swam closer, its powerful form undulating rapidly to counteract the strong current. The reptile raised its head, hissing as its forked tongue sought out its victim.

One Eye could choose to strike the hideous attacker, or . . . lose part of his arm . . . or . . . ! He swung with all his might, cutting a sizable chunk of the willow branch clean through with his sharp blade. He dropped into the cold water inches away from his attacker, but the river whisked him away from the snake's fangs like the pull of friendly paws. Not looking back, he threw his free arm over the willow branch, keeping his head above the frigid water. There was no time to cut the fork of wood tethering his other arm so he steadied himself for the perilous descent. The smaller branches of his life raft bounced off the deadly grey rocks, keeping One Eye safely in the middle of the watery path through the boulders. He lurched from side to side, hanging on for his life. The final torrents of water smashed him without mercy into rocks that bruised and cut his flanks.

One Eye felt dizzy, and his heart pounded rapidly. But as quickly as they had begun, the rapids ceased, and the river slowed and widened out. Shaking with cold and fear but still clinging to the willow branch, he slowly raised his head to see if Pierre was around.

Unexpectedly, he felt a tug and was propelled to shore. Looking behind him, he was overjoyed to see the grey whiskers and dark brown head of the beaver, and his teeth clenching One Eye's willow branch as he pushed him ashore.

Once on the riverbank, Pierre lay close beside the exhausted, battered squirrel, warming him for a while with his body. Noticing One Eye's trapped paw, he gnawed away the wood with his sharp incisors. Once his friend was set free, he lay smiling with chunks of willow bark stuck between his enormous teeth.

"Thanks for the snack, but we'd better get going," he said, while still munching on parts of the branch that had saved One Eye's life. He spoke out of the side of his mouth. "Get on my shoulders. Now, this time, hold on very, very tightly."

"Certainement," whispered One Eye.

༄

This was more like it, thought One Eye as he admired the scenery along the riverbank. Resting comfortably on the back of the hefty beaver, his head supported by that of Pierre, he closed his eye and soaked up the warmth of the sun. After the harrowing, near-death experience of the rapids, they had come to a fork in the river, where Pierre had skilfully navigated across the fast current and made a U-turn upstream into a smaller, slower flowing tributary. This segment of the trip would certainly be more leisurely than his most recent adventure. That was a good thing. A very good thing.

They were heading northeast toward the interior of the Rough Wood Forest and making rapid progress against the weak current.

"Pierre, are you getting tired? We could go ashore and walk for a while."

"Walk! I hate de walking; besides, you can't carry me on your little back."

"Can't argue with that, my friend. Carry on and wake me when we get there."

"Oui, oui, Admiral. Mon Dieu!"

Tullymug Woods

The raucous sound of the giant rabbit's laughter echoed through the forest as he and the young Manorwood creatures warmed themselves by the fire. "You mean to tell me you have no plan! You are just wandering around looking for your father? Ha-ha-ha-ha-ha!"

After their rather tense initial meeting, Smidge, Mash, Marta, Pete and the large rabbit had spent a glorious day gathering food from the forest. Alex had slept most of the day, and with his fever now gone, appeared healthier.

Sitting around the fire for a meal of dry biscuits, cheese, nuts and berries, they were getting to know each other by trading stories. The rabbit, who said his name was Duke, had listened intently and expressed sympathy and anger during Marta's recounting of the savage attack on her village. However, Smidge was feeling foolish and embarrassed by the rabbit's reaction to the explanation of his quest. Mash came to his aid. Rising to his foot paws, he attracted Duke's attention with a tap of his sword butt on the mirthful warrior's paw.

"If it was that stupid, do you think I would have joined him?"

"I don't know—would you?" queried the rabbit between fits of howling laughter. His huge shoulders contracted as he exhaled another guffaw. "It sounds like a bunch of wild tales!"

Anger was rising in Mash's voice. "Look, you giant jumping snowball: Pete and I are Smidge's friends, and we have heard the stories too. Whether his father is alive or dead is not the point! Finding out the truth about what happened to him is." With wet eyes, he abruptly sat down. Marta reached over and put a comforting paw on his shoulder.

Duke sensed a noble warrior's spirit in this young squirrel. He covered his face and coughed into his paws to stifle his laughter and spoke to Smidge in a decidedly more serious tone.

"Humphff, humphff, well, yes, Master Smidge. Tell me more about these tales of your father. What was his name again?"

"Terramboe," replied the earnest young otter proudly.

"So what makes you think he is still alive?"

"It is simple sir: He has never been found dead," Smidge replied quickly.

"That seems rather weak, young man."

"I know," replied Smidge forlornly, "but it is all I have, really. Other than the fact that he was a strong fighter, and well, he wouldn't give up, and well . . ."

His voice grew softer and softer as a confusing mixture of emotions overtook him. "I just want to find some creature able to tell me something, or find a clue. Even if I only find his grave, at least then I would know what happened to my father."

"If you keep heading northwest, you will soon get to Magnath's kingdom and the black rats. Then you and your friends will be in your own graves," stated the rabbit sternly.

"He's not dead," muttered Smidge under his breath as he turned away from the others.

An uneasy quiet settled over the group as each of them munched on the fresh roots that Pete had dug up. Mash had gathered a variety of nuts that tasted exquisite after being roasted on the smoky fire. The cooled mint tea that Duke had brewed washed away their thirst.

Breaking the silence, Pete asked, "What do you know about Magnath and the black rats, anyway?"

Duke's face knotted into a gloomy, faraway look. "I know enough, son, to last me a lifetime." As he spoke these few words, his eyes moistened with large tears.

"I am sorry for asking," apologized Pete, aware that he had saddened the big rabbit. "I just thought maybe you could give us some clues about where to search."

"It's okay. Many seasons ago . . . well, it's just . . . I've been alone out here in the bush so long I have lost touch. I am not sure I can help you." Then, seeing the looks on the young beasts' faces grow more despondent, Duke tried to sound more upbeat. "Hey, but I know a rat who might be able to tell us something."

"A rat! You must be nuts. The only good rat is a dead rat!" sputtered Marta, choking on her tea.

"I am no nut, squirrel-brain," said Duke, laughing at his own joke. "She's a Norwegian water rat, different from these local hoodlums. Miss Marple was shipwrecked long ago and never associates with any other beast. She keeps a house upstream from here, a couple of days' walk from Magnath's fortress. The black rats leave her alone, but she is aware of everything that happens in the Woods of Death."

"Woods of Death?" Everyone was suddenly intensely interested.

"North of here and westward toward Magnath's fortress are the Black Hills. The forests there are filled with slave traders and deserters from his army, so that's what I call them."

Smidge couldn't conceal the excitement in his voice. "She must know something! When can we see her?"

"Well, we'd have to split up, since Alex isn't walking very fast," said Duke thoughtfully. "Mash could stay here and protect Marta and Alex, and the rest of us could leave tomorrow at dawn. We'd be back in a few days."

"I am not going to any Death Woods, no way!" whined Pete. "I'd rather go swimming!"

"Don't pee yourself, Pete. Stay here. I am sure Marta could use your help for something," offered Mash.

"Like being a chaperone for you two lovebirds," wheezed Duke, bursting out in a loud snicker. The two squirrels, blushing like a crimson sunset, scuffed the ground with their foot paws and avoided eye contact, as Smidge and Pete joined Duke in laughter.

Now that the mood was less serious, Pete couldn't stifle his curiosity any longer. "So, if you don't mind me asking, why are you called Duke?"

"Well, laddie, do you see anyone else around? So why not?" Everyone giggled.

"Come on, what's your real name?" asked Marta.

Looking sheepish, Duke hesitated, then muttered under his breath, "Muckross."

"Duke Muckross!" They all erupted into further gales of laughter.

❧

Smidge, who had gone for a short walk, had come to rest on a large, mossy rock poking at a rotten log with a stick. Duke was right. It had been silly to drag his friends into this dangerous, crazy quest. He really hadn't thought things out very well. Yet the strong, desperate need to understand what had happened to his father could no longer be ignored. He would never be at peace until he had an answer. Certainly this wasn't the time to stop! Mash and Pete should break camp and take Marta and her brother to safety. He alone would continue the quest after meeting Miss Marple. His mind made up, he wielded the stick like a sword and plunged it deep into the rotten log before returning to the warmth of the fire.

10

WHERE THERE IS SMOKE . . .

Tullymug Woods

Y ou will do nothing of the sort!" stated Mash angrily. "We are in this together."

The next morning, after a troubled sleep, Smidge tried to explain his decision, but his friends would not accept his idea of them returning home while he carried on alone.

Even Marta joined in, eager to join the quest now that Alex had awakened feeling much better. "Smidge, you and your friends have helped us, and now that Alex is stronger, we want to help you in return."

The young otter was taken aback by the outpouring of support and friendship he was receiving.

Duke sat back, watching, but said nothing. He could see that Smidge was wavering in his decision. Rising to his paws, he spoke directly to Mash.

"I sense you have a brave heart, young beast, but Smidge is right. The Woods of Death is no place for girls and the wounded. We need you to lead the rest to safety."

Mash started to disagree, but the rabbit raised his massive paw to hush him. Gripping Mash firmly on the shoulders, he fixed his eyes on those of the young squirrel.

"It is best."

"Girls!" Indignant, Marta rose to complain.

Mash turned to her, resignation on his face. "He's right. Alex needs us."

Before there could be any further objections, Smidge and the aging warrior rabbit grabbed their packs and departed at a fast pace.

"Well!" said Pete as he curled up by the fire. "That's a lot of walking anyway. I am going to rest up in case there is any fighting."

"You do that, friend. You just never know when we might need a good decoy." Mash was smiling as he reached for Marta's paw. "Okay, let's eat. Then we can pack up."

Pete grunted, closed his eyes and was asleep before Smidge and Duke were barely fifty metres away.

❧

Though it had been raining fairly steadily since Smidge and Duke had left, the morning had been wonderful. Marta and Mash had fallen into a happy rhythm of working together around the camp while they made breakfast. Unable to keep the smiles off their faces, they frequently held paws between chores. Mash found enough firewood and thick leaves protected from the rain by overhangs of rock to construct a roaring blaze to warm them. Marta foraged skilfully for roots and herbs and then prepared a thick soup that smelled so delicious everyone's spirits were lifted. Pete slept by the fire until awakened by the yummy aroma wafting by his nose.

"Oh my, Marta, this soup is fantastic! I think you should live in Manorwood," remarked Pete, slurping loudly. "Can you make candied sweet potatoes?"

Marta looked quickly at Mash and blushed, while Mash kept busy tending to the fire. All Mash could think about the whole time was how surprised his parents would be when he brought Marta home!

Breaking camp, they headed south, enjoying a change in the weather. The sun's warmth made Alex begin to feel better, but his slow pace was making him feel guilty about holding up his friends.

"Don't worry, Alex, the day has just begun, and we are in no hurry," smiled Mash as he turned toward Marta.

"It is a very pleasant day for a walk in the woods," Marta giggled as she reached for Mash's paw.

"You two are starting to make me ill . . . again. I think I am going to puke!"

"Oh, stop it, Alex. Concentrate more on walking and less on complaining." Without bothering to look at Alex, Marta continued to gaze into Mash's eyes.

"Well, I guess I'd better concentrate on walking, since you two aren't even looking at the path to see where you are going!" chimed in Pete.

North of the Valley of Stone

After a night's rest and a hearty breakfast made by Misty, Grunch had led the band northwest out of the valley. None of them had been this far from Manorwood, and the farther they ventured, the more tense their mood became. Each of them remembered tales of attacks on unsuspecting wanderers by masses of rats. So the motley crew carried an assortment of makeshift weapons:

knives, short swords, slings and lances. Eager to find the strays and head back toward the safety of home, their hopes had risen with every hill they crested. But as the daylight had faded, so had their hopes. That night, their spirits had sunk lower as a drenching rain made it impossible to start a campfire.

When they awoke the next morning, chilled to the bone, they broke camp quickly, determined to cover as much territory as possible. A second day of fruitless hunting for the missing young was starting to wear on everyone's nerves. Whenever the weary searchers stopped to rest, arguments erupted about whether to give up or to keep looking. Two older otters were grumbling about their sore paws when Grunch let out a low whistle to caution all the searchers to stop and be quiet.

Gerr used paw signals to indicate to those beasts closest to him that danger lay ahead and to tell everyone to form into groups on either side of his position. Then he whispered, "What is it? What do you see?"

"Down there, see the smoke!" pointed Grunch excitedly from the top of a tree next to Gerr.

"Do you think it's them?" asked some of the otters excitedly.

"I want to be careful, in case it's not." Gerr signalled to the beasts on either side to hold their positions. "Why don't you come with me, Grunch, and you and I will have a little look."

The two crept down the hill, circling downwind to avoid detection. They had to carry their knives in their mouths because the brush was so thick, they needed both front paws to clear the way.

Abruptly, Grunch halted and crouched behind a tree trunk. Paw-signalling to Gerr to stop, he whisked his knife into the other paw. The squirrel swung out to the right around a tangle of fallen logs. Sure that he had heard movement directly ahead,

Grunch scrambled to higher ground to sneak a look. Peering from behind the trunk of an old beech tree, he scanned for danger. He heard the snap of a twig behind him, but before he could react, cold steel was pressed into his throat. Out of the corner of his eye, all he could see was a rusty, battered sword held by a dirty paw. The intense pain in his neck from the tip of the sword told him that, if he flinched, death would be instant.

Foul-smelling breath delivered the harsh warning: "Don't move, squirrel. You fools entered our trap like little babies. Now, don't you be a-crying for your mother or you'll die. Understand?"

Nodding his head ever so slightly, Grunch acknowledged the warning.

"We saw you coming for miles, you and your friends. By now, I am sure me mate has your otter friend, so let's go check." Clucking like a grouse hen, the rat pushed Grunch forward. Hearing a response to his signal, he chuckled gruffly and shoved the prisoner harder.

Within a short distance they met up with Gerr, who was indeed in a similar fix. Grunch had not been able to see his captor's face, but if he was as ugly and mean-looking as the rat who had captured Gerr, then they were in serious trouble.

Gerr and Grunch exchanged nervous looks. Neither was as concerned about their own lives as they were about an interruption to the search for the young ones.

Prodded forward by the sharp blade tip of the rat's sword, Gerr's mind continued to race. Were they fools to be out here searching in this wild, perilous territory? They were so naïve. What did any of them know of the dangers beyond Manorwood? They were so lucky that Terramboe had risked his life to protect their idyllic way of living. Gritting his teeth with determination, he was impatient to find Smidge before he lost another loved one to evil. He glanced over at the grimy, tired face of Grunch. They both had too much to lose to spend any time as captives of these dirty thieves. But before he could gather his wits to confront his captor, a brutal push knocked him to the ground.

&

It took a while for the Manorwood band to realize that Grunch and Gerr were not coming back. Without a leader, chaos reigned. Finally, a hefty otter named Broadtail jumped onto a rock and shouted for silence. Several minutes later, the agitated chatter settled down enough to allow for him to speak.

"Listen up! We can't just stand here and bicker while two of our mates are missing. Come on! Let's go get Gerr and Grunch back! I need volunteers to step forward."

It was almost comical to see the otters and squirrels, young and old, trip and fall over one another as they tried to move backward.

"Go yourthelf, if you want to be a hero tho baaadly," shouted an old crooked-toothed squirrel.

An argument with pushing and yelling ensued between Broadtail and the rest of the band. A rescue did not.

&

Happy banter went back and forth as Mash and his companions continued southward. Shafts of sunlight penetrated the thick canopy of trees overhead to brighten the way. Mash occasionally let the others rest while he took to the treetops to scout ahead. In mid-afternoon, he ran back quickly from one of these scouting expeditions and gestured silently to his friends, telling them to hide behind the stump they were sitting on. Marta was in the middle of checking Alex's wound, and he groaned as she roughly pulled him off the stump and onto the ground.

Mash crouched down beside them and whispered. "There are voices up ahead. Keep quiet and stay here while I circle around uphill and check it out." He ran off before Marta could reply. She lay between Pete and Alex, clutching her uncle's sword in one paw and Alex in the other.

Mash could feel his heart pounding in his neck and his paws trembling with fear. There were angry voices ringing through the clear morning air. At the top of the next knoll, he quickly climbed a spruce tree, carefully concealing himself behind its branches as he ascended to its tip. Scanning the forest, he could barely make out a large group of beasts partly hidden in the shadows cast by a stand of tall aspens on the crest of a hill.

It was impossible to make out what sort of beasts they were, for the wind was not carrying their scent his way. Their shouting and shoving indicated they were most likely evil rats like the ones that had attacked Marta and Alex, and they stood right in the middle of the path to his home in the Valley of Stone. How could he get Marta and Alex around them to safety? They needed a diversion, but what?

Mash returned from his scouting foray and joined his companions, who had crowded together behind the huge stump.

"I can't really tell, but I think it's a bunch of bandits. They're in our way, so we need to divert their attention to get around them. I can draw them away from the path by leading them through the clearing at the bottom of the hill, but I need a head start. So Pete, I want you to crawl up to that rock halfway up the hill and start yelling and banging sticks or something to make a ton of noise. When you see the path is clear, signal for Marta and Alex to run for it."

"Wait a minute! What if all these bandits come after me, not you? What am I supposed to do? Die?" asked Pete angrily.

"Of course not, you hole-hog. Once I show myself, they'll think I made the noise and start chasing me."

"I don't know, Mash. It all sounds so complicated, and Alex can't move very fast." Marta said as she rung her paws together anxiously.

"We don't have any choice. They're blocking the path, and any other way is too difficult for Alex to travel. I'll try to join you as soon as I can."

"What do you mean, try?" asked Marta with alarm.

"It's dangerous, and it will take time for me to lose them. You have to be prepared to travel alone for a while. That's all."

With tears welling in her eyes, Marta gripped Mash's paw tightly. "Nothing is going to happen to you, is it?"

"No way. Soon we will be feasting together with my brother and my parents." Putting his paw on Marta's, Mash continued. "Up the hill, past the aspen trees, the path continues south, all the way to the Valley of Stone."

The two held each other close for a long hug. Alex closed his eyes and muttered, "Hey, you two, I think I am dying and not because I am bleeding. You make me sick! Hurry up!"

"I feel very sick too," moaned Pete, "'cause I *am* going to die."

Mash cast an exasperated glance at Pete, picked up his weapons, and without another word, pushed Pete toward his place in the diversion.

Marta whispered, "Good luck." Helping her ailing brother to stand, she supported him with one arm and shouldered the pack with the other. Together, they awkwardly got into a ready position for the run to the bushes. Looking up the hill, Marta could no longer see Pete. Away from the path, Mash, already poised to be the decoy, nervously pawed the ground.

Marta knew he was too far away for him to hear her curse quietly. "You'd better live through this, or I'll never forgive you, Mash."

☙

Pete was in position and now it was up to him to carry out the next part of the plan. He started pounding two large sticks together, making a loud cracking noise that pierced the still morning air. The bandits immediately went quiet, and Pete assumed they were advancing toward his hiding spot. The closer he imagined they got, the more nervous he became and the harder he cracked the sticks together. Overzealous, he started swinging the sticks like swords and jumped out from his hiding place to face the bandits.

"Don't bother coming any closer, or you risk death!" While uttering his threat, he brandished the sticks in a wild frenzy, but with his eyes firmly shut.

What was Pete doing, running around, waving sticks like he was rabidly insane? In a panic, Pete mistakenly ran toward Marta and Alex.

The plan was in complete ruins! Climbing the closest tree, Mash jumped from branch to branch, tree to tree, with lightning speed. Drawing closer, he suddenly stopped. He couldn't believe what he saw.

"Halt!" Mash shouted as he leapt into the midst of the onrushing horde. He started to laugh. "Guys, it's me, Mash, from the Valley of Stone."

The startled "bandits" banged into one another as they came to a sudden stop. The otters and squirrels stood back in surprise at finding one of their missing young ones.

Broadtail rushed forward. "Glad you are alive, but you sure have some explaining to do."

"Where'd Pete run off to?" asked Stride.

"Back to Marta and Alex, two squirrels we are bringing home with us. They were attacked by rats, and Alex is wounded."

Broadtail pointed at Stride. "Fast as you can go, round up those cowards that deserted. Flash, help Pete's and Mash's friends over here." Broadtail turned back to Mash and placed a muscular arm around his shoulders. "I have bad news for you."

Standing amongst the fallen logs and rocks the Manorwood band was busy transforming into a resting spot, Mash listened intently to Broadtail's news—that Gerr and Grunch had disappeared when they'd gone to investigate a nearby campfire.

Mash was worried about what had happened to his father and Smidge's Uncle Gerr, but enormously relieved to see his friends approaching, unharmed. Flash was lending Alex a supporting shoulder to lean on. As they got closer, Mash ran to hug Marta tightly. Then he punched Pete playfully on the shoulder.

"Pete! What were you doing, swinging those sticks around?"

"It must have been the repressed hero coming out in me."

After everyone stopped laughing, Stride arrived to explain that the others had refused to fight and were returning home.

"Just as well. We need only brave beasts with us now," Broadtail reflected. He turned to Mash to explain the group's inability to agree upon a plan to rescue Gerr and Grunch.

Seething with anger, Mash jumped onto a log to address the group of otters and squirrels from Manorwood. "What have you been doing? What are you afraid of?"

"Settle down, Mash," implored one of the older otters. "We haven't been in battle for a long time and we were . . ."

Mash cut him off. "Well, it's about time, don't you think?" He could feel the nervous energy flowing through him, and even though most of these beasts were his elders, he carried on, speaking rapidly. "Let's form two groups. Pete, you stay here with Marta and Alex." He pointed at some beasts lounging against a large rock, warmed by the sun. "Flash, you and Stride take that group and circle round to the left, then wait for my signal to charge." He whistled high, then low.

"Yes, sir," answered the young otter. Then she flashed her wonderful smile at the beasts still resting against the rock.

"Let's go!"

Too surprised to refuse, the beasts looked at each other and quickly followed.

Even in his excitement, Mash sounded calm. "Broadtail, you and I and the rest will come in from the right, near those rocks." The otter nodded his understanding. "Grab anything you can use for a weapon—stones . . . sticks . . . anything! Let's go!"

The two flanking groups separated to encircle the enemy's campsite. Broadtail and the other otters panted to keep up the pace set by the fast-running Mash. At the top of the knoll, taking cover behind a large rock, Mash held up a paw for everyone to pause. He slowly climbed the craggy boulder and peered down toward the campsite. Then, dropping to the ground, he turned to report.

"I can see the campfire. Get ready to rush them," ordered Mash.

The rest of the group looked reluctant, staring at the ground and stealing nervous, sideways looks at each other.

"Come on, there can't be very many of them," said Mash encouragingly.

One small squirrel cried out, "But I only have a rock, and they probably have bows and swords."

Ignoring the beast, Mash delivered the signal to attack. With the sound of sling rocks crashing through the tree branches, Mash was over the boulder and heading down the slope to rescue his father and Gerr. The rest followed, but some had to be encouraged with a forceful push on the butt by Broadtail's rear paw.

The two Manorwood groups stormed through the trees and surrounded the campfire, but that is all they captured. The campsite was empty.

11

CALL TO ARMS

Rough Wood Forest

The size of the Rough Wood settlement of Castorville amazed One Eye. Most of the inhabitants of this sprawling community were descendants of the original settlers from the Far East Beaver Colony. Lines of log buildings radiated out for quite a distance from the large, sturdy docks jutting out into the river. The smoke of cooking fires wafted slowly toward the woods surrounding the town. The main street bustled with beavers, otters, squirrels and mice coming to trade at the harvest market. The boisterous conversation rising into the smoky air was in a mixture of languages, but mostly French. The aroma of fresh-baked bread mixed sweetly with the scent of sun-warmed herbs. Lining the streets, hawkers chanting their sales pitches stood behind stacks of vegetables displayed on wooden planks; they had to shout to be heard over the din.

On the morning following their arrival, One Eye and Pierre strolled through the settlement, talking loudly over the noise of the merchants.

"We have lots of time before the council meeting tonight. Why don't we get some food and then visit my good friend Lastor. The old coot always knows wadd's a-going on."

"Sounds good to me. Lead the way, Pierre."

One Eye noticed some youngsters playing games with smooth, bark-less sticks. The differently shaped sticks were obviously crafted by strong, sharp beaver teeth. One child threw a stick high into the air, and the rest pushed, shoved, tackled, tripped and wrestled, trying to be the first to get to the stick and bring it back to the thrower. Although it seemed like a confusing pile of bodies rising and falling across the muddy ground, and there was an occasional yelp of pain, everyone seemed to be having a good time.

One Eye and Pierre slowly made their way up the crowded street until they came to a massive lodge, so old that the logs and sticks that built its frame were covered with green and brown moss. The bark, once the white of birch, the pale green of aspen or the brown of hardwoods, was gone, replaced by the black rot of age and smoke. However, the structure itself still looked sturdy, and smoke billowed from the chimney.

Pierre led the way up to the door and entered without knocking. He beckoned impatiently for One Eye to follow him inside.

"Allo, Lastor. It's me, Pierre. Are you here?"

"Come in, you lodge-rat. How are you?" The voice beckoned from the central room, "I am by the fire, trying to keep these old bones warm."

They entered the darkness, nearly colliding with a chair.

"He lives by that fire," whispered Pierre.

"Is there some beast with you?"

"Yes. My dear friend, One Eye the squirrel."

Entering the parlour, his eye adjusting to the dim light of the fire, One Eye could make out the form of an enormously overweight beaver with a pelt heavily tinged with grey. Sitting in front of the stone fireplace, the beast's bottom filled a rocking chair so tightly that One Eye wondered if the beaver could ever get out of it!

"Lastor, this is One Eye One Shot. I knew his father well. He is a good beast." Pierre motioned for One Eye to shake paws with the old beaver.

"Where are you from, One Eye?" Coughing, Lastor gestured for them to be seated on cushions by the fire.

"The Tullymug Woods to the south and west. I have come to ask for your help."

"Slow down, don't rush him," said Pierre softly. "And speak up. 'E's as deaf as a log."

Seeming to ignore One Eye, Lastor spoke directly to Pierre.

"And how is your lovely wife, Giselle? I hope she is well."

"Well enough to keep me busy with a list of things to do that will take many seasons."

Impatiently, One Eye interjected, "We have been attacked, and I seek your help, sir."

Like an irritable schoolteacher, Lastor turned slowly toward One Eye and asked, "Who is we?" Then turning just as slowly back to Pierre, he calmly asked, "Pierre, would you like something to eat and some tea perhaps?"

One Eye was almost beside himself with frustration. "How can you think of food at a time like this?"

"Anytime is fine. Now would you two like to eat or not?"

Finally, One Eye realized that Lastor only did things his way and at his pace. He reluctantly accepted the offer. "Tea and a biscuit would be wonderful, thank you."

"Now, Pierre, you know where to find things. Why don't you go into the kitchen and make the tea?"

Once Pierre had left the room, the obese beaver moved slightly forward on his chair, close enough that One Eye could smell his old age. In a conspirator's voice, the elder wheezed, "I don't like to involve Pierre. He is a terrible meddler. Now, what do you have to tell me? Is Magnath causing trouble again?"

Surprised at Lastor's knowledge of the evil king, One Eye felt a surge of optimism. "Yes, his raiders have attacked us at harvest time many times before, but for several seasons we have been able to move around and avoid his pillaging. This time, he sent an army! We had a battle plan ready and resisted, killing a great number of his soldiers, but we also lost many brave souls and most of the harvest." One Eye rose and paced the floor. "I want revenge. I want to stop him from coming back and killing more of my friends! The harvest is for us to feed our families, not for him to fill his vile, disgusting belly."

"Oh, I agree with that. Magnath deserves a fate worse than death itself. That is why many seasons ago we chose this place as home, far away from that evil kingdom. We do not wish to bring trouble upon ourselves. I do not see what we can do for you."

"Magnath is growing larger and stronger each season. What is to stop him from roving farther into the Rough Wood Forest and attacking you next?"

The old beaver was silent, apparently thinking, lightly tapping his foot paw on the ground. Finally, he spoke, as if waking from a dream. "What is it that you want?"

One Eye stopped pacing and stood before the elder of the tribe, close enough for the beaver to feel his hot breath.

"An army big enough to crush Magnath!" One Eye spoke in a soft, low voice, yet the strength and determination of this passionate squirrel warrior could not be mistaken. The tense silence in the room broke as Pierre returned from the kitchen with a clanking tea tray.

Lastor fiddled with his whiskers and contemplated the surprisingly bold request made by the rash young creature. "What experience do you have in battle, my son? What makes you think you can speak knowledgeably of these matters?"

Not backing down, but rather taking a step forward, One Eye looked directly into the black eyes of the gray-whiskered beaver. "I have seen beasts I love die and I have sworn that this will never happen again. Is that answer enough, sir?"

Lastor was quite taken aback by One Eye's forceful manner and heartfelt emotion. "Well, let me give this some consideration. The fall council meeting is a few hours from now. Pierre, what are you waiting for? For goodness' sake, pour the tea. Now, young man, tell me more about yourself."

☙

About two hours later, Lastor led the way down to the meeting area. One Eye had envisioned a small council meeting of the leaders, perhaps in a meeting hall. He was astonished to see hundreds of beavers, otters, muskrats and water voles gathering in a huge grassy common area just outside of town. The relatively flat open field had a large wooden platform at one side set with chairs and a table.

The street leading out of town and into the field overflowed with a chaotic mass of animals moving slowly forward, shoulder-to-shoulder. The voices of the hawkers rose in shouts and singsong voices above the din as they tried their best to sell the meeting-goers all sorts of wares.

"Fresh alder chew-sticks, succulent fresh growth! Gnaw your way through the meeting with these tasty morsels!"

"Fresh fishheads! Come and get them! Three for the price of one!"

Great! contemplated One Eye. *I get to stand with hundreds of stick-chewing, fish-breathed beasts.* He turned to Pierre with a quizzical expression. "I thought you said this was a council meeting?"

"It is, my son. We include everyone in our meetings. Democracy, you know."

Slowly, they made their way to the platform. After some of the younger beasts helped Lastor onto the podium and into his chair, all the leaders gathered around. Lastor whispered to them for some time.

While they consulted, the crowd started to fill the field. One Eye moved to the side, feeling awkward about not being a water creature, and sat with his back resting against a tree on the edge of the clearing.

Finally, a spokesbeast moved forward to address the crowd.

"Attention, attention, all good beasts of the Rough Wood Forest. . . . Bonjour."

The rest of what the large otter said was spoken rapidly in French. One Eye could not completely understand, despite the fact that he had learned quite a bit of the language on his visits with his father to Pierre and Giselle's home. What he could understand seemed related to matters of no interest to his purpose, and so he began to doze off in the afternoon sun.

Shocked awake when he heard his name being called by Lastor, One Eye gathered his bearings and was embarrassed to see the entire assembly staring at him. Pierre hustled through the crowd and led him forward to the stage.

"Wakey, wakey, mon ami. Lastor wants you to tell the council your story. I will translate for you." After pushing One Eye up onto the stage, Pierre touched the shoulder of Lastor, who was finishing his speech to the crowd.

Wanting to encourage a friendship with the Farlanders, One Eye tried his best French. "Mes amis, mes salutations! Je suis arrivé . . ."

Many of the onlookers yelled out, "English, please!" It obviously pained them to hear him use his poor French, since so many of them spoke very good English.

Carrying on in English, One Eye related the story of the many attacks upon his village and others by Magnath's army of black rats. Finally, he ended with an emotional plea for help.

"We must make a stand against these evil aggressors and put an end to their tyranny. Don't assume you are safe here. Soon they will be burning your villages, killing your loved ones or making you slaves. Please join us in a battle for freedom and honour!"

Many in the crowd cheered approval, but one strong voice asked in a mocking sort of way who would be joining them in this great battle against evil, since he saw only one squirrel.

One Eye, never lost for words, even though he did not yet have a single plan in his head, replied with ferocity. "All Woodlanders. Every peace-loving squirrel, mouse, groundhog, otter and rabbit!" The crowd cheered, and Lastor smiled knowingly at the rest of the elders on the platform.

๛

One Eye felt so nervous about what the council would decide that he couldn't stop pacing the creaky wooden floor in front of Lastor's large fireplace. He and Pierre had been waiting at the old beaver's house for an hour. On the walk back from the council meeting, One Eye had told Pierre that squirrels did not eat sticks or fish, and he had threatened hibernation if they didn't find him "real food" soon. Luckily, they had discovered an undersized stall in the market that specialized in gourmet delicacies, including roasted nuts. One Eye had devoured most of the purchase before they even returned to Lastor's home.

Just as Pierre was about to plead for the tenth time for One Eye to stop making such a racket pacing the floor, Lastor entered the room, moving much faster than he had when he first met One Eye. The events of the day seemed to have invigorated him.

"Well, my friend, you will have your army! The messengers are on their way, and every able-bodied fighter in the Rough Wood Forest will be gathering here and then travelling to join your fighters in the Tamarack Hills."

"Thank you so much!" One Eye felt tears welling up in his eyes. "You have made the right decision."

"Enough, son. You must hasten and gather your troops. We will join you in five days' time at Aspen Meadow."

One Eye was shocked and overwhelmed by the rapid progression of events, especially when he realized he didn't have a clue where to start finding his "troops." What had he gotten himself into?

Before One Eye could speak, Lastor rushed out of the room. "I must have a nap before the feast tonight," he said.

12

INTO THE WOODS OF DEATH

The Woods of Death

The morning had started out sunny, but now dark clouds covered the eastern sky, and a stiff wind whipped leaves at the travellers like arrows. The wind made Smidge's eyes tear, and he found it difficult to keep them open to avoid rocks and branches. Ahead, Duke, more adept at land movement, was clearing a rough trail through the heavy bush. Tirelessly, the rabbit hacked branches with his large sword and pushed aside fallen logs with his powerful rear legs. They had walked at a fast pace since leaving the others at the camp the previous day, and Smidge's legs felt heavy and clumsy with fatigue. On the first day, full of excitement, he had jumped over the lesser obstacles, but after sustaining a few unexpected falls, he now stepped with caution onto even the smallest log or rock.

"At the top of the next hill we'll have a wee gander to see where we are and stop for a bit of food," encouraged Duke.

Between heavy breaths, Smidge replied, "Sounds like a good idea to me. Are we almost there?"

"Ha, laddie, if I knew that, I wouldn't have to have a wee gander, would I!"

"Great! I am following a giant deluded bunny, Duke of Nothing, along a trail that doesn't exist, into oblivion!" muttered Smidge under his breath and tripped on a fallen log. "Ouch!" he screamed through his clenched teeth. "Do you have any idea at all where you are going, Duke? Is this even a path?"

"Of course, it's a grrreat route, but not often used. Besides, any trail easy to find is probably watched by folks you do na wanna meet."

"I'd rather take my chances than get one more branch in my eye or trip every two minutes!"

Without warning, the dark clouds opened up, and the north wind swept in a cold rain that pelted them mercilessly. They were soaked in minutes. Puddles rapidly formed on the ground, and the rocks became even more slippery and treacherous.

"Oh, grrrreat!" muttered Smidge as he pulled himself from the mud after his latest tumble over a wet rock.

"Hurry, I see some boulders ahead where we can take shelter," called Duke, increasing his sword speed to clear a path. But even he was having trouble getting uphill as the ground became a slippery carpet of wet leaves over thick mud. Without warning, the rabbit slipped and became a tumbling boulder of wet, white fur rolling down the slope directly toward the weary otter.

With his head down, protecting his face from the weather, Smidge didn't see the danger until there was no time left to react. The two beasts collided and then combined into a bigger ball, gathering speed, rapidly rolling out of control. The trunk of a mammoth oak tree abruptly stopped their tumbling. Luckily for Smidge, the huge rabbit hit the trunk first, preventing his smaller companion from being crushed against the tree.

Unfortunately for poor Duke, the impact of his back and head hitting the tree trunk knocked the wind and his senses right out of him.

Smidge lay still for a moment to regain his breath and then began to struggle out from beneath the unconscious Duke. Careful not to disturb the injured rabbit, Smidge struggled a long time before he was able to push himself clear. As he rose to his paws, a sinister voice startled him.

"You won't be going anywhere, otter."

The last thing Smidge remembered was a sharp pain on the top of his head and an overpowering urge to sleep paralyzing his body.

۰

With much effort, Smidge opened his eyelids, which felt weighted down by rocks. In the semi-darkness he could make out Duke's bulky silhouette lying beside him, snoring softly. He felt comforted by the big oaf's presence. Rising up on one paw, he peered around and determined that they were in a small cave. Light was filtering in around two boulders, likely blocking an entrance. Creeping as quietly as possible, he peered around one of the enormous rocks. Garbled conversation, spear tips and the tops of heads were all he could make out. He gnashed his teeth in anger and then despair. They were prisoners—guarded by armed beasts strong enough to move these rocks! Making his way back to Duke, he gently nudged the rabbit's shoulder, hoping the big beast was merely sleeping, not still unconscious.

He was relieved when Duke spoke, even though he did so without opening his eyes.

"Can a beast not get a gooood rest without youse a-poking me?"

"Duke, we're prisoners!"

"Welcome to reality, laddie. When did you make that brilliant discovery? You've been sleeping so long I thought I might starve to death."

"What else do you know about this place? Or is it all about food, you herbaceous glutton?"

"Believe me, laddie, it's all about me and my stomach, but more to the point, we have, unfortunately, bumped into a band of slave traders. Fortunately, they feed their captives so they can get a good price when they sell them. The good news for you is that they will most likely choose a younger beast to sell as a slave."

"A slave! Sold to whom?" Smidge stood up, fear transforming his face.

"To Magnath or a slave ship."

"What about you?"

"I am probably tonight's supper. So remember, spit out the tough parts."

❧

One of the large rocks was soon rolled back, allowing sunlight to stream into the cave, temporarily blinding the two captives. An immense rat carried a large, dirty wooden bowl, containing a pitiful portion of awful-looking food. The size of the bowl only made the meagre portion of food look smaller.

"Up on your paws, both of you," snorted the rat, who was quite winded from his effort to move the boulder.

"I think he's sick. I can't get him to wake up," whimpered Smidge, stepping back from the motionless form of the large rabbit lying on the cave floor.

"He's only going in the stew pot, anyway. But then again, I suppose that depends on what he's sick from. Let's see if his stomach hurts," shrugged the guard, bringing his leg back to kick Duke in the gut.

Just as the large rat's leg started its forward arch, Duke rolled on his side and grabbed the leg, catching the guard off balance. With a huge push, he launched the surprised beast backward. The villain's collision with the rough rock wall knocked him out. At the same time, Smidge tripped the next guard as he rushed in to investigate the commotion. The rat stumbled forward and was brought to the ground by a blow from the outstretched arm of Duke. When he hit the floor, Smidge jumped on his back and hit him as hard as he could with the dinner bowl.

Propped up on one elbow, having never risen from the ground, the huge rabbit surveyed the two unconscious guards and smugly commented, "Not too baaad for not even getting out of me bed, is it laddie!"

"Yes, but we'd better get out of here fast before the guards are missed," squeaked Smidge, his throat tight with excitement.

"Aye, laddie, you got that right."

The two escapees stood with their backs pressed against the wall of the cave opening, waiting for their eyes to adjust to the daylight. Not seeing any threat, they slowly ventured down the stony path, scanning for more rats.

"Over that way! Hide behind that boulder near the big oak tree. Quick, and keep low!" directed Duke.

Crouching as far down as he could, while trying to avoid tripping over the rocks that scattered his path, Smidge scurried to the hiding place. Duke, waiting until Smidge was hidden, used his powerful rear legs to bound high over the boulder. Before he landed, a crescendo of urgent voices rose from the area of the cave, announcing the escape of the prisoners.

"Now, laddie, why don't you escape while the going is gooood, eh? Use that path over there beyond those bushes. I'll keep a lookout for trouble. Run as fast as you can. Now get going!"

"What about you?"

"I'll be right after you. Hurry up. My growling stomach will give us away."

Off scampered the otter as fast as he could, skidding on the gravel path as he rounded the bushes. The shower of small stones raised by his paws made a sound just loud enough for an observant guard to notice.

"Over there! The otter is escaping!" With surprising speed, the rat took up pursuit, rapidly advancing on Smidge with every stride. Realizing the danger for his young companion, Duke stretched out his leg into the path of the guard.

The surprised rat went sprawling across the stony earth. "It's the rabbit, get him!" he managed to squeal as the air rushed out of his lungs when he crashed to the ground.

Duke turned and ran in the opposite direction of Smidge to draw away the young otter's pursuers. The plan worked well—so well that an angry gang of rats quickly surrounded the wily warrior.

"Well, boys, what a surprise to meet all of you out here in the wild woods of the north." Slowly turning to look at each rat with a lopsided grin, he said, "You've done gone and spoiled me walk. You won't mind, then, if I . . . kick a few of you in the head?" Abruptly rising on his hind legs, Duke leapt high in the air. Spinning with rapid-fire kicking, he struck down three bandits before they knew what was happening. The unlucky rats fell to the ground, startled.

But unfortunately for Duke, the remaining rat had his sword ready, and when the huge rabbit landed slightly off balance, the sword tip came to rest precisely on his chest.

Wobbling on one paw to prevent himself from pressing harder on the sharp blade, Duke resigned himself to a second captivity. "Well, this is a grrreat way to ruin a fine outing."

Smidge's legs were burning with exhaustion, but when he looked behind him he saw no one in pursuit. Somewhat relaxing his running speed, he cast an eye over the dark forest landscape for somewhere safe to rest. Spotting a protected hollow, he dove in headfirst.

After resting for several minutes to catch his breath, he grew anxious waiting for Duke. Lying on his stomach, he peered over the brim of the earthy bank for any sign of his jolly friend. A powerful wave of fear and loneliness caused his mouth to go dry and made it impossible for him to concentrate. He slid down into the leaves at the bottom of the hollow and turned onto his side. Too tired to cry, he just lay there, his arm over his eyes, and wondered if his father, during his ordeal, had felt as desperate and alone as he did right now.

❧

Smidge was tired and hungry. He had waited for Duke for what seemed like hours, but there was no sign of his friend. The realization that he was on his own had forced him to clear his mind of self-pity and start to think about what to do next. Should he head back and find out what had happened to Duke? Forge ahead and see if he could find Miss Marple? Or try to find Mash, Pete, Marta and Alex?

None of these options seemed particularly promising, so he continued to lie in the bed of dry leaves, paralyzed by indecision, watching the high wind currents push white, grey-edged clouds across the sky. The air felt cool, but it was very comfortable when the sun appeared between the clouds to warm him. Shortly, he fell asleep.

Soon, his slumber became restless. The dream unfolded the same as always: cool autumn night air, battle noises, screams and the pounding of paws running into the darkness of the forest. Fear. Sounds and images drawn in his mind from the night his father chased away the attackers. Then nothing. There was never anything after that. Just nothing.

✌

Smidge could feel the warm sun on his face as he lay on a soft bed of pine needles, leaves and twigs. Restless, he started to wake, but was unable to keep his eyes open and the heaviness of sleep descended upon him again. His body soon felt like it was floating, and he could sense his father's paws on his back, pushing him into the air.

Smidge had always loved it when his father lay on his back with his legs extended, bouncing him up and down on his paws. Totally trusting, Smidge would stretch out his arms and legs, yelling with delight as he was tossed high into the air. One evening, he had slipped off and crashed to the ground. When the air had returned to his lungs, he had screamed at his father.

"You dropped me!" Tears ran down his cheeks.

Terramboe had never done well with tears of any sort.

"Come now, son, I did not. It wasn't far to fall. You couldn't possibly be hurt, so stop whining and be brave."

Smidge had wailed and wailed until his father lost his patience and walked away. Thinking his father couldn't really hear him, he had whispered, "I hate you!"

His father had turned and stared at Smidge, his eyes filled with sadness.

That was the night that Terramboe had gone out on patrol and never returned. It was a horrible way to remember the last time he had ever spoken to his father, and his father would never know how hard he had tried to be brave that night. He wanted that moment back, but the dream was always the same. He could feel his lips moving. "I don't hate you, I don't."

"That'th good, Mithter, but who are you, Mithter? Hey Mithter," said a cheerful voice.

Smidge felt a small poke in his ear.

The baby voice whispered, "Wake, wake, Mithter! You just gonna lie there talking to yourthelff?"

Smidge was suddenly wide awake. He was startled to see a little grey-brown mouse using the full length of his tiny arms to prop Smidge's eyelid open and staring very closely into his left eyeball.

"Well, are you, Mithter?"

"It was a bad dream. I guess I can thank you for waking me up."

"Okay, Mithter, but why you theeleapin' in a pile of weafes?"

"Why not? . . . Actually, I am lost."

"Weally! What are you doin' here, anyway?"

"I am looking for my father."

"Heck, tho am I, and my mother too. They went out to get thome food and they never came back. I've been wooking all day. Hey, Mithter, maybe you can help me and I can help you!"

"Unless you know where to find a rat named Miss Marple, or can show me where my long-lost father is, or find my friend Duke, captured by slave traders, then I don't see how you can help me." The frustration of the situation seemed to overcome Smidge. Closing his eyes, he rolled away, his back toward the little mouse.

"Mithter, Mithter. I can help you!"

"Sure, sure. Now just go away and leave me alone."

"Look, Mithter. You can lie here until you are thomebody's dinner. But I am the only fwend you have wight now, and I can help you."

"Okay, how?"

"I know that rat you were a-talkin' about—Mith Marple."

Smidge opened his eyes, his heart filling with new hope.

"Really! Where?"

"Just wollow me, Mithter." Jumping onto Smidge's shoulder, he pointed the way.

"Follow?" asked Smidge incredulously.

"Well, Mithter, you are way bigger than me, so just wollow my finger," replied the mouse, as he settled in for the ride and pointed west.

The wee mouse, Matty, proved to be an excellent navigator through the thick underbrush and fallen logs that seemed to stretch on forever. Soon Smidge and his chatty little guide arrived at a clearing on the edge of a gurgling stream. Huge red pine trees encircled the clearing, and tall golden grasses swayed in the breeze descending from the mountains.

"You stay here and hide. I will go and tell Mith Marple I bring you. Thee don't wike thurprises."

With that warning, Matty jumped out of the woods and confidently strode toward the door of a ramshackle cabin tucked into the side of a small hill on the far side of the clearing. The wooden door looked to be the strongest part of the construction; it appeared to be the only thing holding up the log sides, which were leaning at very odd angles. Heavy curtains covered the windows, and the grass roof was drooping down so far that soon the entire structure would be hidden.

Carefully climbing the stairs of the porch, Matty's small figure was dwarfed by the brightly painted red and yellow door. The mouse knocked loudly and then jumped back, as if afraid of being attacked.

The door burst open, and the most bizarrely dressed rat Smidge had ever seen sprung out, wielding a large broom. With her "weapon" poised over her head in one paw, and her eyes shielded with the other, she searched the clearing. The fierce, pirate-like poise was made much less fearsome by her bright, multi-coloured summer dress and floppy red hat. The headwear, sprouting at least fifty pigeon feathers, sat askew on her large head.

Smidge could tell from the uncoordinated wandering of her eyes that she must be blind.

"Who's dere, and what des youse want?" she screeched loudly.

"Oh, hi, Mith Marple, itth juth me, Luke'th thon, Matty."

"Matty, youse parents are very upset. Dey look for youse everywhere. Dey be down by da river, now. Dey be worried sick youse drown."

"I will go find them wight away, but ferth, I wath wondering if you could help my fwend, Thmidge."

"Who is he and what des he want?"

Smidge had moved up behind Matty, once he had determined the rat must be blind. "I am an otter and . . ."

"I can smell dat," the rat replied, staring somewhere past Smidge's left shoulder.

"I wondered if you knew anything . . ."

"I know every-ting about what goes on around here. Every beast stops here to trade information and to taste my potato wine or enjoy one of my pigeon scones. What youse want? Every-ting costs, ya know."

"I want to find my father. He might have been captured many seasons ago by slave traders or Magnath soldiers and brought back this way. He is a large otter and he was possibly wounded."

Miss Marple stroked her chin and put the broom up against the wall. "How much is it worth to ya?"

This lengthy negotiation was making Matty nervous, and he was eager to reunite with his parents. "Hey, Thmidge, if you ever come thith way again, thtop by. Thankth, Mith Marple, but I'd better be on my way." With that, he jumped off the porch and ran toward the river.

Smidge felt despondent. "I really don't have anything to give you, Miss Marple."

"It don't matter anyway. Ever since dem slave traders come with dere boats, beasts just disappear." Ignoring the young otter, she grabbed the broom and started to sweep.

"Please, I am just a son looking for his father."

Pondering this for a moment, her mood softened. "Well, I do believe I might know some-ting. In trade, maybe youse could do a little work for me, hey? My eyes are no good and my bones are all stiff with de arthritis, especially in dis cool autumn weather. Up

on top of dat cupboard is my winter hat. Youse fetch dat and I'll tell youse 'bout your pa."

"Okay, anything!"

"Any-ting!" she cackled, shuffling inside the dark cabin and sitting down on a rickety wooden chair. "Well den, after youse be a-finished with dat, I need da garden weeded and some potatoes dug. Den I be a-tellin' youse about your pa."

Smidge hurried through the jobs as fast as he could. He rushed to retrieve the hat so he could get outside into the fresh air. The cabin air smelled sour from the odour rising from piles of garbage and food scraps strewn everywhere. He had an open mind, but maybe everyone was right to call them dirty rats.

Once he finished filling the basket in the garden, he placed it in front of the old rat, who had fallen asleep in her chair.

"Excuse me, here are the potatoes."

"Oh, yes, well, now I suppose youse be wanting me to relate da story about your pa. Okay, one day a band of Magnath rats was a-passing by, comin' back from one of dem foraging trips. Dey was very excited about da prize dey were goin' to give da king. Lots of reward, dey thought. Well, it turned out to be dat dey had captured demselves a big otter. Da king likes strong slaves 'cause dey be able to do lots of work. Dey took him right up dat path yonder. He smelled scared."

"Is that the way through the mountains to Magnath?"

"Yep. It be da only path through around here dat I know of."

"Well, thank you. I'll be off now." Smidge jumped off the porch and started toward the path.

"Hey, youse be crazy to be a-going dat way! Don't youse want some food?"

The thought of eating anything from that foul-smelling cabin turned Smidge's stomach, and the thought of his father being a captive, slaving for Magnath, made his stomach even sicker. Without a reply, he started to run toward the path through the forest covering the slopes of the mountains that rose toward the fortress. Then, feeling scared, he turned back. Maybe he should find Duke? Uncertain, he ran back and forth until he couldn't move another step and then dropped into a pile of leaves and started to sob.

❧

Two large rats escorted Duke down a narrow, rocky path.

"Move along, Jack the Rabbit," taunted the largest guard as he prodded Duke with his spear. He had a crooked, bumpy nose and missing front teeth and his foul breath soiled the frosty air as he snarled. "We haven't got all day, fluffball. Hop along now."

The other guard snickered in encouragement. "You tell him, Knuckle Nose."

13

Old Enemies

The Woods of Death

Smidge had fallen asleep in the woods beside the steep, twisting path to Magnath, but his uneasy rest was broken by the sound of gruff voices. He lay still under the blanket of leaves and moss that had been his hastily made bed.

"Get your paws moving, you fluffball! With that kick of yours, you're worth more to us alive than dead, but don't tempt me, rabbit."

Two despicable-looking rats were prodding a large figure along the rocky pathway. The rusty ends of their lances had left a brown-red tattoo across the beast's back.

Smidge, being careful to stay hidden, crawled through the undergrowth toward the voices. It was Duke! The brawny form of the enormous rabbit was unmistakable. The slave traders were taking him to Magnath!

Smidge's first reaction was to hide until the group had disappeared farther up the path, but the sight of his friend so tired and defeated was too much to bear. Hadn't Duke saved his pelt? Didn't he owe it to Duke to stand up and fight? But another glance at the nasty-looking rats quickly brought him crashing to reality. There was no way he would be able to defeat those scoundrels without a cannon strapped to his back. Yet, he couldn't let another soul be enslaved by Magnath! Dejected, he slipped back behind a tree and closed his eyes to think.

Gradually, a smile spread across his face. He started to sneak through the forest ahead of the travellers, only stopping at a small spring to smear mud on his face and pick up three smooth stones.

"Hey, bunny rabbit, want a carrot? Hey, Knuckle Nose, did you ever hear the one about the rabbit with no tail?

"No, Bad Tooth. How's it go?"

Bad Tooth starting bringing his sword up over his shoulder, squinting with one eye to line up his blade with Duke's tail and grinning a wicked, toothless grin. "Like this, ha ha ha."

Just as Duke started to tense in anticipation of the blow, the villainous rat was distracted by a crazy-looking creature walking along the trail toward them.

"Who goes there? Stop now and answer me," demanded Knuckle Nose.

Smidge carried on, shambling toward the group on the path, muttering to himself until he was about five meters away. "Hello there, my fine beasts. I am just returning from Magnath where I gave the king a fine display of my juggling talents." He nodded at their prisoner. "Oh, I say, his majesty will love such a big, fine beast for his slave collection."

"Shut up, blabbermouth, or you will be going back to Magnath with him," snarled Knuckle Nose.

"I don't believe him. Make him show us his 'talent,' chirped Bad Tooth.

"Yeah, let's see this show of yours, Mud Head, and it better be good or you'll be joining our little group—as a slave."

Duke watched this strange beast very carefully. Something in his voice seemed familiar. Yes, that was it! Smidge had told him about his juggling. What in the world was the little otter up to?

Smidge moved closer and started tossing the rocks into the air in a skillful display of juggling. The rocks ascended in perfect half circles that rose higher and higher and faster and faster. The three rats stood motionless, mouths open, mesmerized by the rhythmic movement of the flying rocks. Duke kept his eyes focused on Smidge.

"Now, for the finale, gentlemen: the high flyer!" With that, Smidge tossed up two rocks and then heaved the last rock up as far as he could.

The rats extended their necks back to watch.

The instant the first two rocks landed in his paws, Smidge threw them as hard as he could at the slave traders, knocking Knuckle Nose senseless and dazing Bad Tooth.

Seeing the rocks strike, Duke propelled himself through the air, knocking down Bad Tooth and landing across the fallen rats, pinning them to the ground. Trying to dodge the final rock, Smidge dove onto the jumble of bodies heaped on the path, but not before the projectile struck him on the bum with a dull thud.

"Ouch!"

Duke started to laugh. "Am I ever glad to see you. You are quite the juggler!"

"Then what are ya laughing at?"

"That final rock must have hurt your butt!"

"Actually, that's better than usual. The last one usually knocks me out."

They both laughed until they were crying. Hearing the groans of the rats brought them back to the present moment.

"Free my paws, and we'll use the rope to tie them to that tree," instructed Duke.

"Not so fast," growled a rough voice from behind them.

"What you got, Jimmy?"

"Well, Slim, if I's not mistaken, it's a bunny sandwich right here on the path."

Slim pushed forward for a closer look. "Oh, I get it. Otter on top, bunny in the middle, and hey, isn't that our mates Knuckle Nose and Bad Tooth on the bottom?"

Their joke was interrupted by the cries of two prisoners Slim led by a thick rope.

"Smidge, is that you?"

"Uncle Gerr, what are you doing here?"

"We've come to rescue you."

"Bbbbbb-puth-puth, that's a good one," sputtered Duke, seeing the captives with their tightly bound paws.

Jimmy shoved Smidge aside roughly and kicked Duke in the ribs. "Shut up, bunny. At least the others live to be slaves. You are dinner."

Knuckle Nose and Bad Tooth were moaning loudly but roused themselves enough to push their way free from underneath Duke. "Yeah, let's eat."

Tullymug Woods

One Eye trudged through the deep grassland of Muddy Moss Moor into the forest, where he could travel faster, from treetop to treetop. Even though the trip downstream on Pierre's back the day before had been uneventful compared to the previous trip on the big river, he felt exhausted. After a brief reunion with Ting, who was recovering nicely from his wounds in Giselle's care, he had set off this morning to find his 'army.'

He smiled to himself as he remembered his friend putting on a brave show of walking around the cabin to show that he was strong enough to come along. Giselle had stood behind the wounded mouse, rolling her eyes and shaking her head to convey her strong opinion that Ting was not ready in the least. One Eye had kindly told Ting to rest up while he gathered the troops, because his help would soon be needed to plan the battle.

Ting had told him of several possible hiding places for the Woodlanders, but when he found them, they looked as though they had been undisturbed for seasons. The hours were ticking away toward the day of the rendezvous with Pierre and the Farlanders. It seemed futile to search the entirety of the Tullymug Woods by himself, so he had headed into the Tamarack Hills to seek assistance from old friends.

Resting on the stout branch of a maple tree, he hungrily devoured some of the wonderful nut loaf Giselle had packed for him. Wiping the crumbs from his face, he was readying himself to continue his search when a low voice nearly startled him off his perch.

"Well, you one-eyed tree-hugger. Where have you been? We all thought you had died in the battle."

Emerging from the branches of a bushy spruce tree, a strong, lean flying squirrel named Long Flight glided effortlessly onto a limb of the maple tree. The webbing at the base of his arms and legs where they met his body acted as wings when he stretched out his limbs, allowing him to glide silently from tree to tree. Long Flight was aptly named due to his amazing flying ability: not only could he cover long distances, but he often embellished his flights with aerial stunts like flips and spins before executing picture-perfect soft landings.

"The rumours of my demise are greatly exaggerated, you flying freak!" replied One Eye, chuckling.

After greeting each other with a short hug and slaps on the back, One Eye's manner quickly became serious. "Where are the Woodlanders of Muddy Moss Moor? Have you seen any of my clan?"

Long Flight's shoulders dropped. "Many died or were captured, One Eye. The woods have been very quiet these past few days. I hear tell that a few Woodlanders fled to the caves nearby. As for your clan, I don't know of any that survived. They fought bravely, allowing the others to escape. I am sorry."

The news forced One Eye to sit down in an attempt to control his rapid breathing and pounding pulse. With tears in his eyes, he looked up and stared intently at Long Flight. "Will you and the rest of your kin help me revenge the death of my clan?"

The flying squirrel looked uneasy and glanced away. "You know that the Flyers don't fight. We have no weapons. I don't think it is even worth asking the clan for help. We are sorry for your loss, but if we fight Magnath we will only bring trouble for ourselves."

"You think you're safe, hiding up here in the hills? It's just a matter of time before Magnath's evil reaches out and strikes you too!"

"I don't know, One Eye. So far, Magnath has shown no interest in the few chestnut gatherers up here in these hills."

"Don't be a fool! Besides, have you no feelings about what happened to my friends? These were beasts that you knew and traded with! Are you Flyers heartless?"

The emotion in One Eye's voice stirred something in the heart of the Flyer. Turning his head, he returned his friend's gaze.

"Perhaps we can help you without actually fighting. I'll have to ask the rest."

"Excellent! First, we must find the remaining Woodlanders. Then we have to gather as many fighters as we can, because in three days we have to meet up with the Farlanders at Aspen Meadow."

"The Farlanders?" exclaimed Long Flight.

"Yes, they too realize that no beast is safe from Magnath and that the time to act is now!"

"Ok, let's get going!"

The two squirrels exchanged stories of recent events as they traversed from tree to tree, one jumping powerfully from branch to branch and the other effortlessly gliding and occasionally spinning 360 degrees before landing two trees ahead. After a lightning-fast trip through the treetops, they arrived at the home of the Flyers. Priding themselves on their love of heights, the flying squirrels had built their entire community in the peaks of some of the tallest trees in the woods. "The taller the tree, the longer the flight" was their motto.

Wasting no time after their arrival, Long Flight took One Eye to meet the leader of the clan, Flyboy. He quickly agreed that the Flyers should help in any way they could other than by fighting. The call for an urgent meeting was hollered through the treetops, and soon everyone was gathered at the base of a huge maple tree.

The Flyers were chattering loudly. Arguments and intense discussions had broken out the moment Flyboy informed the clan of the news and the urgent need to help.

"Let's go fight some rats!" yelled an eager young squirrel named Treetop.

"We don't fight!" one of the elders stated loudly.

He was quickly shouted down by a group of younger clan members impatient to have some action. Flyboy raised his voice to explain his idea for compromise.

"I agree we must help our brothers and fellow Woodlanders against the forces of tyranny. But I believe we can show our support by providing aerial assistance in non-combat roles, such as reconnaissance and communications."

"No! We want to fight rats!"

"Yeah, me too. Give me a sword!" screamed Breezer, another of the younger squirrels.

"Now, now, I admire your courage, Treetop and Breezer. But even if we were to decide to fight, we haven't got time to train you. We have to meet up with the Farlanders in just a few days. Let's concentrate on what we know how to do—fly."

Undeterred, the younger squirrels began chanting, "Fight! Fight!"

"Stop that racket, youngsters. You do not know the horrors of war like I do," interrupted an ancient, grey-whiskered squirrel. Walking stiffly from the back of the gathering, where he had quietly been watching the proceedings, he motioned for silence. As the sole survivor of the Great War, Lech always commanded respect from his fellow Flyers. Although crippled by age, his wisdom and experience were often called upon.

He proudly wore his military flying suit, although it no longer fit him properly. The specially designed garment had built-in armour and extra webbing under the arms, allowing for longer flights. It had been used in the Great War between the Flyers and the Grounders.

Many seasons ago, the Flyers had wished to expand their territory southward into the lush woodland occupied by the Grounders. A vicious war had ensued, and many lives had been lost on both sides. When the two sides had declared a truce, after many months of battle, the combatants had been surprised by how easy it was to work out a compromise. The Flyers had paid heavily for their aggression and had made a vow to never wage war again.

Once the old warrior had everyone's attention, he simply said, "Flyboy is right. We can do much to help our friends without having to fight."

A murmur of agreement went through the crowd; however, not every beast accepted the decree. Some of the older beasts were still bitter about the long-ago feud. "Yeah, I am not dying for them," muttered many of the older clan members.

Eventually, the majority of the Flyers agreed to help, but not fight. Spoiling for a scrape, Treetop and Breezer showed their disappointment by scuffing the ground with their paws, turning on their heels and leaving.

Flyboy barked out orders. "We have no time to spare, Flyers. Treetop and Breezer, get back here. You're in charge of getting the supplies, and Long Flight, you pick five volunteers to help you find our fellow Woodlanders. Tomorrow morning, we move out. Let's get ready!"

One Eye suddenly felt very tired. He had watched nervously from the rear of the crowd, perched on a branch, while the Flyers debated. Now the excitement of the past few days took its toll. With his back leaned comfortably against the trunk, his eyes began to close. All he wanted to do was sleep.

Long Flight was worried his friend would fall off his perch.

"Come on, One Eye, you lazy Grounder, let's get some food. Then, tonight, we can decide on the best way to help you win the battle."

The Woods of Death

After a quick search of the empty campsite, it became obvious Gerr and Grunch had been abducted. It took a few moments for the discouraged Manorwood creatures to recover, but without prompting they all began to search urgently for clues as to the direction taken by the kidnappers. A trail of broken twigs and disturbed ground cover led them into the thickest part of the forest. Coming upon a worn path heading northwest towards the Woods of Death, they continued tracking the kidnappers for three days, energized by Mash's determination.

On the afternoon of the third day of their search, Pete was getting tired and labouring hard to keep up with the others. But he was the first to smell a campfire and the aroma of food.

Having volunteered as scouts, Broadtail, Mash and Marta edged down the slope through the thick underbrush. They could hear voices, but before they could see a thing, Marta stopped abruptly and grabbed Mash's shoulder, pulling him to a halt.

"It's them. I would recognize those voices anywhere."

"Who?" whispered Mash, puzzled.

"The rats who almost killed Alex and me." She turned and headed back the way they had come.

"Where are you going?"

"To get my sword. Those rats are going to pay dearly for what they did."

Broadtail and Mash had no choice but to hurry after her. After a brief conference, it was decided that the mistake of carefully approaching the rats would not be repeated. They would attack quickly, hoping for surprise.

Once he learned who the kidnappers were, Alex insisted on joining the attack. "I wouldn't miss another moment of Marta the Marauder in action!"

Puzzled by the comment, Mash gave Alex and Marta an enquiring look before rushing off.

Crashing through the brush, Mash could see rats sitting in a small clearing around a roaring fire. To one side, he could see his father, Gerr, Smidge and a large rabbit tied to a tree. Not stopping for a second, he raised his sword and charged. The beasts behind him fanned out to surround the campfire.

Alerted by the sound of cracking branches, the rats jumped to their paws, lances and swords at the ready. Mash hurdled himself over a log and landed on the edge of the clearing. The rats, outnumbered, stepped backward and placed the points of their weapons on the chest of the nearest prisoner. The onrushing Manorwood beasts stopped in their tracks, while the rats smirked.

"Well, good day," spat the biggest of the rats through his yellow-stained teeth. "Nice of you to drop in."

"Release them now," growled Mash.

"Or what, kiddo?"

A wicked smile slowly formed on Jimmy's mouth as Mash hesitated. Looking around at the ragtag "Warriors of Manorwood," he laughed. "What are you sorry lot going to do about it, anyway, eh?"

Mash charged forward, but Broadtail, sensing a fatal outcome for the prisoners as well as the rats, spread his arms and stopped the young squirrel from attacking. Behind them, the ordinarily peace-loving beasts began to form ranks, moving closer together with their weapons drawn, as anger began to replace their own fears.

Seizing the moment, the scar-faced rat began negotiating.

"Calm down, you 'fierce' warriors. No beast will get hurt if you throw down your weapons. Then, all of youse move over to that oak tree there and face the other way except youse two," he sneered, gesturing at Broadtail and Stride with his sword.

"Youse two, put all the weapons by the fire. After youse done that, youse can join your friends and count to fifty. We'll be long gone, so don't youse try and chase us, or we'll kill this old squirrel." With that, Knuckle Nose pulled the blade of his knife tighter against Grunch's throat, causing him to gag.

"Not so fast," spoke a voice from behind the ranks of Manorwood beasts. Slowed by helping Alex down the steep slope, Marta had just arrived. She stepped forward with her sword held high.

Shock swept across Slim's and Jim's eye-patched faces, pushing their opposing good eyes wide open. "Not you again!"

"Yes, unfortunately for you." Before her words were complete, Marta stormed across the forest floor, wielding her sword.

To every beast's amazement, the two robbers went crashing through the brush in a mad dash to escape. Mash and Broadtail raised their weapons and launched themselves at the remaining rats, but these two, dismayed by their mates' desertion, took flight as well. Marta chased after Slim and Jim, while Mash rushed to the captives and cut their ties.

Sensing that his son wanted to run down the villains, Grunch took a firm grip of Mash's paw and said, "Let them go, they are just worthless thieves."

After a moment, Mash started to relax and brought his gaze down to his father's eyes. He saw them filled with tears.

"Thank you, son. You are very brave."

"You would have done the same for me, Dad."

The rest of the Manorwood beasts flowed into the campsite, cheering raucously. Marta, satisfied the villains were vanquished, returned from the chase. She held Alex's paw, and they both watched the joyful reunions. Grunch had his arms tightly around Mash, and Pete kept thumping Smidge on the shoulder.

Everyone in the Manorwood band was hugging everyone else and jumping up and down with excitement and relief. Finally, Mash and his father approached the two squirrels from Brookside.

"Dad, this is Marta and her brother Alex." Smiling broadly and giving Marta an admiring look, he added, "Or should I say, Marta the Marauder!"

Despite the happiness around him, Duke stood back from the crowd, looking wary and uncomfortable.

"What's the matter, Duke?" asked Marta, moving closer to the fidgeting rabbit.

"I am not used ta so much company. I have been alone a long time."

Before Marta could reply, Grunch extended his paw.

"Greetings, friend. I am Mash's father. I am hearing nothing but good things about you. I want to thank you for helping the young ones."

"Not a problem. You have a good son there in Mash, loyal and brave. You should be proud he is helping another excellent son find his father," said Duke, starting to warm up a little.

"Well, I am not so sure about their brains. It's been a bit of a dangerous escapade."

"Ahh, they're good lads, and we can be thankful they are both safe, and you too."

Dry wood fuelled the fire, and everyone settled in for food and rest. Smidge's recounting of his harrowing adventures and his meeting with Miss Marple left the group enthralled.

Duke remained silent throughout the exciting account until Smidge started talking about his plan to return to Magnath, using the route he had discovered.

"I told you, laddie, you are in need of a lot of help to go anywhere near that evil place."

"Well, with the help of my friends, I'm sure we could find a way to sneak in and . . ."

"No!" interrupted Duke as he leapt to his paws and started pacing by the fire, obviously upset. "I've tried and it's no use!"

"What are you talking about?" asked Pete.

Seeing Duke was upset, the young ones came closer to hear their friend's low whisper.

Trembling with emotion, tears running down his cheeks, Duke lowered his head. "A very long time ago, I lived in the most beautiful warren with my Violet and thirty or so fine beasts. One day, the black rats came and wrought destruction and left nothing behind but death. In the melee I managed to escape, but just barely. The rats herded up Violet and several of my close friends to take to Magnath as slaves. I followed them, hoping to free them, until I saw the huge dark walls of that evil monster's fortress. I knew once Violet was inside I would never see her again. I went crazy. Six rats died by my sword, but just as I reached for her, I took a sword in the shoulder and another in my side. They left me there to bleed to death."

The friends sat in stunned silence. Mash, Marta and Pete looked blankly at the ground, but Smidge stared intently into Duke's eyes with a look of understanding. *So this is why Duke helped me*, he thought.

"The last thing I saw was Violet being pushed through the mammoth wooden gate of the fortress. I carried on, but I don't know why. I had nothing left to live for. I was powerless against that evil that took away my wife. I've lived here, alone, ever since. You'd need an army to get inside those walls."

❧

After a long evening of storytelling and boasting of their bravery against the rats, the Manorwood band was fast asleep, including Broadtail and Stride, who were supposed to be on guard duty.

Pete was dreaming a most pleasant dream, a groundhog dream . . . a groundhog-who-hadn't-had-a-decent-meal-in-days kind of dream. He was running like the wind, faster than his best friend, Smidge (definitely a dream)! Sneaking into Mrs. Festerbug's garden, they had dug up bunches of big, juicy carrots. They were enjoying the crisp sweetness of their first bite when the ever-vigilant gardener had detected the trespassers and let out a grunt of disgust. Startled, they had bumped heads as they looked up to see Mrs. Festerbug's enormous, apron-clad figure charging down the garden row toward them. Dropping their treats, they had almost tripped each other in their haste to escape. As Pete slid under the fence and began running fast along the dirt trail, he could sense Mrs. Festerbug's paws about to grab him . . . and then a brush of air across his face startled him awake.

His eyes opened in time to see something amazing glide by . . . a squirrel. A flying squirrel! He had never heard of such a thing. Drifting back to sleep he muttered, "Do you believe that? A flying squirrel!"

"Well, you'd better believe it, 'cause you're looking at one."

Pete came to his senses slowly as a paw persistently tapped him on the shoulder. Opening his eyes fully in the dim light of dawn, he was startled to see a reddish brown squirrel standing over him. "Who are you?"

"I am Long Flight of the flying squirrel clan. Are you the leader of this band? I have an important message."

"Ahhhh . . . not me. Smidge, Mash, wake up! There's a squirrel here—a *flying* squirrel—to see you!"

Pete's voice was so loud and shrill from excitement that he woke up every beast. Mash had heard tales of the war with the Flyers from the Tamarack Hills and warily greeted the visitor.

"Hi, I am Mash. What brings you so far away from home?"

Long Flight's rapid answer came out in one long breath. "I have been sent to gather as many volunteers as possible to form an army against Magnath. The black rat army has been killing and stealing from all of us for too long. The Woodlanders have been viciously attacked; the few survivors have no food for the winter. That wicked warlord is sending his troops farther and farther away from his castle to pillage innocent, hard-working beasts. My clan and the Farlanders know it is just a matter of time before we are his next victims. Together, we are preparing an attack on the castle to put an end to this tyranny once and for all, but we need help."

Smidge responded with passion in his voice. "We are from Manorwood and we are well aware of the evil deeds of the rats! We have not been attacked for some time, but our Woodland friends, Marta and Alex, have just lost their entire village to that tyrant. We will gladly join the fight!"

A murmur of nervousness went through the air as many of the Manorwood beasts worried out loud about the dangers of battle and being away from home any longer. Their clan had lived in peace for so long, and many of the younger ones had never raised a weapon until now. Suddenly, all the bravado from yesterday's easy victory over a few mangy rats disappeared.

Marta couldn't stand it. "Listen up! I know you don't think this is your battle, but if it had not been for the bravery of one beast, Terramboe, Smidge's father, your village would have been laid to waste long ago. What have you done since? Nothing! You have not experienced the pain of the rats' brutality first-hand, like Alex and I have. You have not seen everyone you love lying dead, everything you have ever known reduced to smouldering ashes, and every dream for the future smashed. Yes, my brother and I seek revenge for the Woodlanders. Fair enough. But, the brave Farlanders have not been attacked, and yet they are fighting because they know this evil has to be stopped!"

Absolute silence had fallen over the group.

After surveying the Manorwood beasts with an intense stare, Marta turned to Long Flight and spoke in a low, measured tone. "Count me in!" Then, she reached down beside her pack to where her large sword rested. With a smile, she looked at the awestruck beasts and asked, "So, do any of you care to join me?"

Smidge said nothing, but jumped up and placed his paw on Marta's, and together they hoisted the blade high over their heads.

Mash looked on in admiration of Marta's bravery and knew he truly had met the girl of his dreams. "I am in!" he shouted.

Alex was filled with wonder at how well his sister had spoken. Although he felt a renewed determination to seek his revenge, he also realized there was more at stake than just his personal vendetta. "Me too!" he roared, suddenly feeling much stronger.

Pete had never been one to take lightly the idea of placing himself at risk, but he was so moved by the passionate speech and Smidge's spirit that he shook his clenched paws in the air and screamed, "Down with Magnath! Here's to the Manorwood Brigade!"

With that, everyone burst into a long cheer of approval, which caused tears to well up in Marta's and Alex's eyes.

Pete and the otters and squirrels all gathered closer to Long Flight to hear more about the plan. After an intense discussion, Gerr and Smidge shook paws with the flying squirrel, promising to meet up with the Farlanders and Flyers in two days' time with as many volunteers as possible. Long Flight described the best route to Aspen Meadow and promised to check in with them during their journey to ensure they were on the right trail. Then, the Flyer scurried up the highest tree, launched himself onto the air currents, and soared northward. The magnificent sight brought out a cheer from the admiring Manorwood Brigade.

Energized with hope, Smidge stepped forward, the first to speak. "Okay, everyone, we have no time to waste. Let's fill our stomachs, get as much rest as we can, pack up camp and be ready to leave early tomorrow morning. We have a long journey and a hard battle ahead of us!"

Shocked by the change in Smidge, the rest stood gawking. The last time they had noticed him, he had knocked himself out with one of his juggling sticks. They were shocked at this change in his demeanour.

Gerr moved beside his nephew. Placing his arm firmly around Smidge's shoulders, he spoke firmly. "You heard him. Let's get cracking. There's much to be done!"

Once the commotion settled, Smidge sought out Duke, who was sitting by the fire, alone.

"Did you hear the news?" he exclaimed, as he sat beside his friend. "The Farlanders, with the help of every beast we can muster, are planning a massive attack on Magnath."

But the large rabbit did not reply.

"Duke, it's the help we've been looking for!" said Smidge excitedly.

"No, Smidge, it's the help you need. It's not my battle anymore. I have long since given up any hope of seeing Violet alive again. Slaves don't live a long time in Magnath."

"But won't you help me?" pleaded Smidge softly.

"I thought I could, but the last few days have shown me that an old beast like me would be of no help. Besides, do none of you understand what you are up against? If you attack Magnath, there will be much death and suffering . . . and for what, Smidge? If your father was made a slave of Magnath, he was worked to death a long time ago. Just go home, all of you, to your warm beds, and keep your ideas of bravery and heroism as dreams." With that, Duke turned away and faced the fire, vigorously poking the embers with a stick.

14

GAME ON

The Woods of Death

It was difficult to leave the big rabbit sitting alone at the campfire the next morning. Duke had been briefly cheered to see that Alex looked healthier after a good night's rest, but otherwise, he remained quiet. Each time Smidge glanced his way, he could see Duke staring into the distance with a forlorn look upon his face. Although sad to part ways with his friend, Smidge was eager to join the other beasts as they prepared to leave for Aspen Meadow. It was the chance he had been waiting for to find his father.

When the Manorwood Brigade started off on the trail to rendezvous with the Farlanders, Smidge held back. Returning to Duke, he gave him a long hug. "I know you don't agree with our decision, but wish us luck."

Duke responded warmly. "Good luck and be safe, wee one. Come back and visit your old friend someday, laddie." The smile left his face, and a distant look returned to his eyes as Smidge left.

Not turning to look, Smidge silently joined the brigade, and for much of the morning walked alone, contemplating Duke's warnings and the dangers that lay ahead.

He noticed that most of the younger members of the brigade did not share his serious mood. They bounced along the trail with enthusiasm, playfully battling large weeds and small trees. As they dashed forward, with swords lashing out wildly, many a milkweed or goldenrod plant fell, savagely cut to shreds. The energy of the younger beasts was contagious, and the older beasts began pairing off to practise sword work and sling-shooting.

There was only one near catastrophe, when an ancient sword, made of a straight shaft of rusty iron and a poorly made wooden handle, had come apart. After a vigorous swing, the blade twirled through the air with a deadly, whooshing sound. At least five beasts had to dive for cover, fearful of being decapitated. The errant weapon struck one of Gerr's foot paws in the midst of a spirited duel with Grunch. The unexpected blow caused him to trip, and he lunged forward with his sword aimed directly at Grunch's throat. A quick defensive parry by the big squirrel avoided a fatal neck wound.

"What in blazes are you trying to do, Gerr? Kill me now so I won't have to worry about dying in battle?" cried out Grunch.

Gerr was about to explain when a rush of brigade members, coming to see if the two elders were injured, drowned out his voice.

"Are you all right? Are you cut?"

"I didn't mean to!" cried a voice from the back.

The young otter, Stride, looking rather unnerved, stepped forward to explain how the blade had become a low-flying missile.

"It's all right, son." Gerr stooped to pick up the crude blade. "But if you think you are going to survive a battle using this rusty old thing, well . . . you need a weapon that can stand up to the powerful swing you obviously have. Now, I just happen to have a small, but sturdy, spare blade that you can use. You can return it when we are both safely back at Manorwood."

"Thanks, sir. Those rats had better be scared now!" And off he went, eager to practise with his nifty new weapon.

Toward Aspen Meadow

The journey through the forests to Aspen Meadow lasted a day and a half and was difficult at times. Jagged rocks cut deeply into paws, branches scraped faces, and fatigue from the constant marching eventually began to wear down the enthusiasm of the troops. As they marched on, there was less talking and laughing, less running and sparring, and it became more difficult to get the otters out of any stream they passed.

Profound water deprivation was evident when they reached a wide river that flowed down through the rocky foothills. No sooner had the otters smelled the water than they rushed ahead and dove in with whoops of delight. The squirrels sighed and curled up in a nearby pine tree. Pete surveyed the river, groaned and lay down in the tall grass on the near bank.

Smidge and the other otters started a game of otter tag, racing underwater at terrific speed. When Gerr was "it," he cut through the cold, dark water, deftly avoiding a submerged log, tagged Stride and twisted sharply away to avoid being tagged back. Just before zigzagging behind a large rock, he spotted something unusual. When he probed in the murky depths, he recoiled in horror as his paw touched fur. Breaking through the surface, he called out for help. With the assistance of several others, Gerr was able to bring the sodden form to shore.

"It's a squirrel! He must have fallen in and drowned," cried Grunch.

"The current in this river is fast, and squirrels can't swim very well," offered Flash.

"I suppose," replied Gerr slowly, "especially with an arrow in his back." He turned the poor creature so that every beast could see the shaft.

Cries of anger filled the air. "Whose arrow? Why?"

"The black rats', that's whose." Gerr angrily pulled out the arrow and held it aloft for all to see its black feathers and red markings.

Silence fell over the group like a suffocating blanket. The faces of the younger creatures plainly showed they had never seen death this close before. None of them had ever been this scared in their lives.

Smidge looked in the direction of Magnath. "Now you see what we are up against . . . why we must end this. Let's keep going."

Collecting their things, they prepared to resume their march on the other side of the river. The otters, who had easily traversed the waterway, waited impatiently on the far shore. The squirrels used a natural bridge created by the overlapping branches of two trees that had fallen from opposing banks.

The brigade was ready to move on when Smidge realized Pete was nowhere to be seen. Crossing back over the river, he scanned the high grass for his friend. Just audible over the noise of the flowing water, he could hear sobs. Following the sounds of distress, he found Pete sitting with his legs drawn up under his chin, weeping.

"What's wrong, Pete?"

"That's the biggest, strongest river I have ever seen!"

"I am sorry, Pete. I forgot you don't like water, but you are too heavy for the branches, so there is no other way across. Let's go, and I'll swim beside you."

"You don't understand," Pete started to wail. "That drowned squirrel . . . I am always frightened . . . I never want to see . . . "

Smidge couldn't understand the rest because of Pete's sobbing. "I know it's sad, but we have to get going!"

"I hate the water. Finding that squirrel makes me think about my brother!"

"Your brother? What are you babbling about?"

"When we were young, my baby brother and I were playing hide-and-seek by the river. When it was my turn to search, I found my brother in the water. His paw was trapped between two rocks, and the current pulled him below the surface. I tried to save him but I couldn't. My parents came and pulled him free. Dad tried to squeeze the water out of his lungs, but it was too late. He had drowned. I have nightmares about finding . . . well, like that squirrel!" Pete hugged his knees tighter and moaned.

"I thought your brother died of a sickness. Why didn't you tell me any of this before? I am your best friend."

"I was ashamed. I tried to save him but I couldn't. It was my fault he died because he was my little brother and I was supposed to look after him. I still feel horrible. You love the water so much, and I didn't want to spoil our fun by telling you. It was easier to just let you tease me."

Smidge put his arm around the groundhog and whispered, "I am so sorry. You were very young, and it sounds like you did everything you could. You are a good beast. Now you need to be strong, and you can be! Look how you helped save Marta. That must have been so difficult for you. After what you just told me, I realize how incredibly brave you are. Right now, we are all frightened, but we will find ways to deal with our fear, especially if we work together. Come on, I'll swim right beside you. You'll be alright, Pete." He helped his shaking friend to his paws, and they slowly made their way to the riverbank.

Pete only hesitated a moment before the two friends waded into the current. Feeling a surge of water cover his snout, Pete gasped and breathed in a mouthful of cold water. Sputtering, he started to flail his limbs in panic.

Smidge, swimming on his back, thrust his powerful tail under his friend's chin and upper chest to lift Pete's face out of the water. They stayed locked in this formation all the way to the other side.

Once they were safely ashore, the groundhog paused and waited until Smidge rolled himself dry in the tall grass. Then Pete shook with all his might, spraying cold water all over Smidge.

As he walked away from the river, he gave his startled friend a good-natured push on the shoulder.

"Payback," he said.

They looked each other in the eyes for a moment and then smiled briefly before joining the others.

Aspen Meadow

The mood was sombre as the Manorwood Brigade marched toward the rendezvous point. No beast spoke, and there was no more swordplay, as they individually contemplated the dangers that lay ahead. The stirring words that Smidge had spoken over the grave of the unknown squirrel reverberated in their minds. They realized, as they trudged over the stony path that wound through the thick pine forest, that some beast might soon be giving a eulogy for one of them.

It was not long before they could smell campfire smoke and hear voices ahead. Emerging from the dark forest, they could hardly believe their eyes! The blazing sun was bathing a huge meadow with brilliant light. As far as they could see, there were campfires and all manner of sleeping shelters. The entire scene teemed with otters, beavers, groundhogs, rabbits, mice and squirrels, busy cooking, sewing and sharpening blades.

When they approached the camp, a squirrel sporting a black eye patch advanced toward them, followed by a large beaver and a mouse with a heavily bandaged leg.

"You must be from Manorwood. Welcome," said the squirrel. "My name is One Eye One Shot—One Eye for short—and this is Pierre of the Farlanders and Ting of the Woodlanders."

"Thank you. I am Smidge of Manorwood. This is Gerr, my uncle, Grunch and Mash of the Valley of Stone, and Marta of Brookside. We and our companions from Manorwood have come to join in the fight against Magnath."

"Excellent! Now please come and rest and eat, for we will be leaving in the morning. Camp anywhere you can find a space."

As they prepared to make camp in a small area on the edge of the larger encampment, the younger members of the brigade found themselves feeling intimidated by the other fighters. The Manorwood beasts could see that, compared to themselves, the other beasts were a well-organized army. Nearby, the Farlanders practised with lances, swords and knives, grunting as they struggled to topple each other, while overhead, arrows whistled through the air, thudding into their targets with great accuracy. The Manorwood beasts were ashamed of their inferior weapons, and their practice sessions, which had consisted of cutting down weeds, seemed childish. They were distracted and could barely organize themselves to make a campsite.

Meanwhile, the commanders of the Farlanders' practice signalled a break. The troops placed their imposing array of weapons up against tree trunks and ran back into the field, swinging long sticks. Several of the Farlander otters passing by sneered at the brigade. In voices easily overheard, they wondered what possible use these scruffy newcomers would be in a fight.

The Farlanders divided into two teams and started passing around a pine cone that was carefully wrapped in grapevine to make it bigger and more ball-shaped. They used sticks with a curved end to give them better control when striking the ball. The object of the game seemed to be to hit the ball between two large poles stuck in the ground in the other team's end of the field.

The wild game captivated the Manorwood Brigade, and they became keen spectators.

Smidge could not stand still. The otters' insults were generating a slow burn in his mind. Finally, he couldn't take it anymore. "Come on, let's challenge them to a game!"

"What? Are you crazy? We'll be slaughtered!" bellyached Pete.

Paying no heed, Smidge moved out into the field and approached the Farlanders. Irritated at the interruption, the beasts reluctantly stopped playing.

"Jouez-vous au hockey?" one asked in a snobbish manner.

Recognizing the blank looks on the faces of the Manorwood beasts, he started gesturing with his paws, inviting them to play.

Smidge nodded his head to indicate "yes." Pointing first at his group and then at the Farlanders, he challenged them to a game.

The otter smirked and simply said, "Oui."

Several of the younger otters and squirrels among the Farlanders gave up their sticks to the newly arrived beasts.

Pete, having duly noted the amount of running involved, volunteered to be the goalie.

At the faceoff, the Farlanders generously allowed Broadtail to take the ball, and he swept it over to Smidge. The otter quickly made a beautiful, long pass to Stride, who with blazing speed ran toward the Farlanders' goal. Winding up with everything he had, he blasted a shot. There was a resounding thud as the ball struck the stomach of the huge beaver that was goaltending. The stunned beast fell to the ground, moaning, and Smidge easily flicked the ball between the posts for a 1–0 lead.

Once the goalie recovered, the game resumed in earnest. Using Stride's and Flash's speed, Manorwood was able to repeatedly move the ball into the Farlanders' zone. Mash scored another goal on a long shot that bounced off at least three players before dribbling between the goalie's legs. Marta, trying to stop a strong young otter named Trouter from rushing the ball downfield, launched herself at the beast's legs and torpedoed him to the ground. The angry beast jumped to his paws, eager for revenge, but Marta was already running the other way, pushing the ball deftly down the field.

Frustrated about falling behind, the Farlanders started to knock the Manorwood players to the ground with thunderous body checks when they came anywhere near the ball. When Broadtail complained, the Farlanders just shrugged their shoulders. Consequently, the Manorwood beasts assumed body slamming must be part of the game. Brushtail, a young squirrel, eagerly hurled himself at several opponents. Eventually, he charged at a burly Farland beaver who didn't even notice when the small beast hit him and slid to the ground, winded.

Soon the score was 3–2 in favour of the Farlanders, and tempers were getting very short. Taking a quick water break, the Manorwood beasts threw themselves down in exhaustion and frustration.

"That's enough! They keep knocking me down every chance they get," complained Stride.

"I'm tired, and my paws hurt. I've had enough hockey," added Flash without her famous smile.

Smidge's competitive spirit would stand none of that.

"Gather 'round! Look, we can beat these guys. Pete, no more playing goalie, I want you to stand in front of their net. There is no way any of them can move you. Marta, grab a shawl and wrap it around you like an apron—you are our new goalie. When they close in, ready to shoot, flap it up and down as hard as you can. Mash, stay far to the left, Stride, all the way to the right, and I will take the middle with Broadtail. Flash and Brushtail, you play back. Let's go!"

Until then, the Farlanders hadn't noticed a girl had been playing, so vigorous were Marta's efforts. However, now that she was wearing an 'apron' she became the target of mocking gestures and snickers of laughter.

From the ensuing faceoff, the nimble Trouter ran past Flash and closed in on Marta with a clear breakaway. Just as he started to wind up for his shot, Marta shook her 'apron' fiercely. The distraction was enough to cause the otter to aim his shot directly into the middle of the shawl.

Obviously irritated by her tactic and remembering the earlier trip by the young maiden, Trouter kept running toward the net. Not slowing, he rammed his shoulder into Marta, sending the small squirrel to the ground, covered almost entirely by her apron. The rest of the Farlander team started to howl with laughter. Seeing the ball resting in the middle of the 'apron,' Trouter tried to flick it into the net, repeatedly jabbing Marta in the stomach with his stick. Furious, Marta's paw shot up, grabbing Trouter's stick so hard that he cartwheeled over her into the net. Now, it was the brigade's turn to laugh.

Mash recovered the ball and starting running up the centre of the field. A huge otter lumbered after him, attempting a takeout, but when he put his shoulder down, Mash jumped over the attacker and carried on. He tried the same manoeuvre over the next attacker, but while in mid-air a second otter levelled him. Before he came to a body-jarring thud on the ground, he managed to push the ball toward Smidge on the left wing. A Farlander stormed after him, but Broadtail cut in and smashed into the beast. The melee that erupted created enough distraction for Smidge to whisk the ball into the Farlanders' zone.

Smidge saw Stride on the far side of the field, charging toward the goal. About to make a pass, Smidge hesitated. He could see an opening between the goal post and the shoulder of the enormous beaver net-minder. An opposing beaver charged toward him, forcing him to hurry his shot, and he fired.

The shot was a rocket and accurate! However, Smidge could see from his vantage point, lying flat on the ground with the beaver on top of him, that the goalie had blocked the attempt at the last second. Striking the goaltender's arm, the ball had rolled toward Pete, who stood in front of the net. He was involved in a ferocious battle with two Farlanders who were attempting to push him away. None of them noticed the ball lying at their paws. In the mayhem, Stride arrived from the right wing at full speed and neatly flipped the ball over the fallen goalie to tie the score.

The Farlanders looked angry and even more determined as the Manorwood players celebrated their goal. While the teams were regrouping for the face-off, Pierre called out that it was

time to get back to weapons training. Both teams agreed to call the game a draw.

The young otter who appeared to be the captain of the Farlander team approached Smidge with an outstretched paw.

"My name is Jean La Truite, but you may call me Trouter. Great game. You play hard. When we first saw you we didn't think you were ready for battle, but maybe you'll be alright after all." Casting a cynical eye at Marta, he continued, "But I am not so sure about little squirrels."

"It was a hard fought game, thanks. Hey, your English is good!" answered Smidge.

"Mais oui. Now we will teach you a little French and how to fight!"

After a long and hard training session, everyone was hungry. Luckily, the meal that night was a feast! They all ate with vigour, thinking it might be their last good meal in a long time.

The Manorwood Brigade sat with young otters and beavers from the Far Woods, alternately eating and re-enacting some of the better plays from the game. As they became more comfortable with each other, they started laughing and telling stories about themselves. Smidge juggled sticks but didn't try the usually unsuccessful finale. Several Farlanders stood shoulder to shoulder, dancing and making faces, while a beaver named Marcel sang a song in French. The ending, when the dancers pushed Marcel backwards over the crouching Trouter, made the Manorwood beasts roar with merriment. This was despite the fact they hadn't understood a single word of the song!

The elders interrupted the frivolity for an early bedtime because of the long march ahead. Reluctantly, the creatures made their way to their beds. All but Smidge, who was pulled aside by Pierre and asked to come to One Eye's campfire.

"Welcome, young man. I trust you have had lots to eat. Please sit with us while we discuss our plans." One Eye, who seemed to be the beast in charge, gestured to an open space by the fire.

Sitting down on a log, he stared intently at Smidge and then addressed the gathering. First, he introduced the leaders: Ting of the Woodlanders, Pierre of the Farlanders and Flyboy of the Flyers. The Flyers had been able to find all the surviving Woodlanders. The mice, moles and squirrels able to fight had been integrated into the Farlanders' battle group. Pierre and Ting would each lead their troops into battle, but overall command had been given to One Eye. The Flyers would perform scouting and communication tasks for the entire army.

One Eye continued. "We will march hard all day tomorrow, starting at first light, and then all the next day. It will be a difficult passage through the mountains to Magnath, but it is a route that will give us the best chance to arrive undetected. Once we reach Red Oak Hill, just to the east of the fortress, we will rest briefly. Pierre, please continue."

The large beaver stood to address his audience. "From information we have gaddered about Magnath, dis will not be easy. One Eye, Ting, Flyboy and I 'ave devised a battle plan. We will go over it quickly tonight and again in more detail before we attack."

One Eye resumed. "Smidge, your efforts to find your father have shown you to be determined and brave. We asked you here because we need to request something very special of you." Clearing his throat and switching his gaze from the fire directly into the young otter's eyes, he continued.

"We need a two-pronged attack for our plan to work. We want you to lead the Manorwood Brigade through the passageway Miss Marple told you about. By attacking Magnath from the south, you will draw their attention as we strike from the east. Grunch and Mash will help you command your troops. To represent the Manorwood Brigade, Gerr will travel with us. What do you say?"

Smidge started to tremble. He wasn't sure if it was from fear or excitement. This was what he had been waiting so long for, but the thought of actually having to fight scared him. In the end, he showed no hesitation. "Yes, I accept. I am honoured."

"Excellent!" exclaimed the rest of the leaders. Gerr stood, put his arm around Smidge's shoulders and squeezed him proudly. Over the last few days, he had marvelled at the change in Smidge's confidence. He was maturing into a fine young beast.

One Eye waited for the emotion to settle and then got right to business. "Smidge, you and your troops will have a longer journey than the rest of us. Since you will not arrive until the middle of the night before the battle, I will give you your orders now."

The long meeting had exhausted Smidge. Heading off to bed, he felt as if he would never sleep again until this was over. The excited young beast imagined finding his father shackled in some dungeon. He longed to see the wonderful look on his father's face when he realized his son was there to free him. Maybe the next time he did sleep, his father, Terramboe, would be sleeping next to him.

15

ATTACK AT DAWN

The Valley below Red Oak Hill

The united army of the Farlanders, the Flyers and the Manorwood Brigade marched relentlessly toward the dark, threatening presence of Magnath. Because Alex was still recovering from his wound, he and Marta journeyed with the Farlanders, who would travel a shorter route than their Manorwood friends.

In the early morning of the second day the main army approached Red Oak Hill. The leaders decided to camp in a valley near a small stream, where the surrounding hills offered excellent concealment from the fortress. The good camping spots and fresh water buoyed the spirits of the soldiers. After trudging from dawn to dusk for two days, it was a huge relief to soothe their bruised and bleeding paws in the cool water. While some creatures made soft beds of pine boughs, others, too exhausted to care, flopped to the ground and fell fast asleep. To avoid giving away their presence, no fires were allowed. Nuts, seeds and chunks of bread sufficed for nutrition.

The Flyers scouted ahead, soaring from treetop to treetop, searching for danger. None had been found so far. The mighty Magnath's overconfidence was about to cost him dearly.

Flyboy gathered his scouts upon their return. Listening to each report carefully, he was able to begin drawing a map to present to the other leaders at that night's meeting. Treetop, who had just returned from his scouting sortie, was still breathless. "One hundred metres before the main gate is a guard house atop a hill. There are at least fifteen rats stationed there. It will be difficult to avoid being seen coming from almost any direction."

"We must not allow them to raise the alarm before the main attack," said Flyboy.

"That sounds like a job for the Flyers," added Long Flight eagerly. "We could easily make a surprise air attack from the trees to the northeast!"

"No, we are not here to exchange blows," responded Flyboy. But Long Flight's eyes burned so fiercely with the desire to fight, Flyboy could not resist adding, "Unless there's no choice."

One Eye's messenger interrupted the discussion to summon the Flyers' leader to the war council.

❦

A small candle was the only light to illuminate the map as One Eye, Ting, Gerr, Pierre and Flyboy crowded around a stump that served as a table. The sketch on the tattered parchment made the obstacles to obtaining victory less frightening. The Flyers' initial description of the immense walls of stone crowned by numerous guard towers teeming with black-armoured rats had made their task seem impossible. The fortress seemed less imposing when drawn on flat paper.

One Eye cleared his throat. "Well, my friends, we have come this far. Now is the time to end the evil rein of Magnath!" Murmurs of agreement rose from everyone's lips, and they began planning in earnest.

South of Magnath

The Manorwood Brigade was still marching, even though the sun had long ago shed its final rays. Smidge fortunately remembered the first part of the passageway through the mountains toward Magnath. When the unknown portion of the trail began, he raised a paw for the brigade to stop.

Grunch and Mash scouted ahead and returned sooner than expected with the news that Magnath was not far ahead—just two more twists in the serpentine path. Finally, the goal was close! The conclusion to Smidge's quest was about to take place, and tomorrow there would be answers, good or bad. He motioned the brigade forward, and they crept quietly through the darkness to find a suitable spot to begin preparations for their assault.

e⁄ɔ

One Eye laid out the battle plans, giving each commander his final instructions. "Flyboy, I want all the Flyers who are not doing message duty to stand by in the trees, here." He pointed to the woods north of the fortress. "Pierre has chosen a platoon of Farlanders to secure the guardhouse. Once they lower the flag, Smidge and the Manorwood Brigade will begin the diversion. Then, we will commence the full attack. Any questions?"

Grim nods of understanding were exchanged, and the leaders silently and slowly returned to their campsites.

One Eye called back Ting. "My old friend, you are the best archery leader I have, but are you sure your wound is healed enough to fight?"

Ting smiled. "You don't pull a bow string with your leg. I wouldn't miss this for anything." Grinning, the mouse then turned to join the others.

The leaders passed by tired soldiers who were wide awake, nervously sharpening their knives, swords and arrow tips. Suitable slingshot stones had been gathered from along the stream bank. Ash saplings straight enough to be arrow shafts were stripped of all branches and sharpened. Intent as they were on the tasks at hand, thoughts of loved ones filled their minds, stoking their longing to be safely at home.

Fortress Magnath

On the south side of Magnath, in the middle of the night, the Manorwood beasts finally reached their destination. Having found a good vantage point, most were making hasty preparations for battle. Others were trying to grab a few minutes' rest before dawn. There had been no time for making a camp. The exhausted beasts had scattered to lay down anywhere the least bit comfortable.

Resting against a log and sharpening his sword, Mash thought of tomorrow's combat but was interrupted by daydreams of Marta and the life they would share together. Smidge thought only of being reunited with his father. Food was on Pete's mind—piles of it.

At the Farlanders' camp, Marta had also mused that night about the plans she and Mash had talked about every waking moment they had been together. Sometime before dawn, she awoke and stared at Alex, who was fast asleep. Reassured that this was the healthiest he had looked since suffering his wound, she quickly fell back into a deep slumber.

Pierre smiled in his sleep and moved closer to Giselle, his gentle snoring filling the night air.

One Eye was awake, worrying that his plan would not work and his friends would die. He had not slept a wink that night.

⁊

It was still dark when the Flyers circulated among the troops, waking the beasts with a tap on the shoulder. Most had already awoken with their mouths dry with nerves. They silently armed themselves and formed into their designated groups. The Flyers, the first to leave, had the task of establishing observation positions and lines of communication back to One Eye's command post, situated in a huge red oak tree on the crest of the valley. They carried stones for self-defence only.

Next came the deployment of the Farlanders' first platoon of otters, led by Trouter. Their mission: silence the guardhouse. The otters were armed only with their knives and slings, so their speed and stealth would not be compromised. Accompanying them was a young mole, Pip of the Woodlanders, who had been the fastest digger in the last harvest feast competition.

Pierre watched them depart. "Bonne chance, mes amis."

Trouter's platoon paused at the edge of the forest that bordered the meadow surrounding Magnath. Sensing no danger, they started out into the open field. While they stayed low to the ground, the early morning mist flowed over them, covering their approach. The otters quickly made their way to the base of the guardhouse, where Trouter slid along the cool, stone wall and peeked around the corner toward the main fortress. The only entrance into the guardhouse was a small wooden door in full view of the guards on the fortress wall. It would be impossible to force entry without being detected, but they had another plan. Quietly, he returned to the others.

"Okay Pip, go to it."

The little mole furiously dug at the base of the stone wall with his huge digging claws. During last night's scouting mission, the Flyers had noticed a jagged crack in the wall just above the spot where Pip was digging. While Pip excavated, Trouter dug away at the remaining mortar around the loose stones with his knife. If they could remove several large chunks of wall they hoped to have enough space to gain entry and surprise the rats inside.

After ten minutes of furious work, they were able to remove two small stones and one large boulder. Combined with the hole Pip was now digging, they had created enough clearance to enter. The young mole hurried back to the safety of woods, while Trouter crouched and eased himself into the dark hole, his knife between his teeth.

Groping blindly, he promptly felt the cool dampness of a stone floor just above him. Had they opened a passage into a quiet, unused area, or . . . ? He raised himself up into the darkness, knife at the ready. He paused to let his eyes adjust. He heard nothing. Good, they had their first bit of luck! Quietly, he climbed into the room with the rest of the attack party silently following. The musty-smelling chamber seemed to be a storage area. A stout wooden door at the far end appeared to be the only way out. Good luck was now replaced by bad. The heavy door had no handle and was firmly secured from the other side.

&

Treetop, Breezer and Long Flight sat in the trees to the north, waiting for the flag to drop on top of the guardhouse. Their job was to observe the battle and take turns reporting back to One Eye. When minutes ticked away with no signal, they become more and more anxious. What was taking so long? They had seen Pip scurry back into the woods ages ago. Had the otters been detected and slain? Since they heard no alarms raised by the rats, they concluded that Trouter's squad must be trapped.

"Grab your biggest stone and one other and leave your sling pouches behind. We have some flying to do!" ordered Treetop. The other two young Flyers needed no encouragement. They had been hoping for this all morning—battle!

Bracing himself against a branch, Treetop pushed off as hard as he could. Soaring silently into the morning air, he adjusted his flight path toward the top of the guardhouse, where two rat guards stood at their posts on either end of the roof with their helmets off, half asleep. Treetop launched a stone like a missile. The stone thudded on the head of the guard and the rat was dead before he hit the ground. Long Flight banked sharply and fired his own missile, striking the other guard on the upper chest and knocking him backwards onto his arse. With his mouth gaping open in surprise, the rat looked up just in time to have his toothless orifice jammed forever open with a stone dropped by Breezer. Any warning the rat had thought of delivering was silenced.

Skidding to a landing on top of the guardhouse, the three Flyers grinned wildly at each other with excitement. Pressing themselves along the stone wall, they snuck down the stairs at the far end of the roof.

Halfway down, they froze as they heard the boisterous voices of the rats at breakfast. The slurping and smacking sounds of the eating rats rose toward them from an open door at the base of the stairs. Suddenly, they were filled with fear as they realized they had no weapons other than a few stones.

They waited, but no one came toward them. The clatter of plates and forks mixed with the occasional grunt meant the rats were too busy eating to notice anything. The Flyers quietly slid by the dining room into a hallway around the corner. They paused to orientate themselves to Trouter's entry point. The best choice seemed to be a series of doors down the corridor, well away from the noise of the rats. Several were open and empty but the two at the end were bolted shut.

Edging along the wall, they stopped and wrestled with the heavy bolt on the first door. Sliding back the crude metal rod, they laboriously pulled the heavy door open. Their senses were immediately overpowered by a horrible rancid odour. With tears in his eyes, Treetop quickly closed the door. *Putrid rats*, he thought. *Who knows what's in there? Maybe it's where they keep dessert!*

The next door was double-bolted and even heavier than the first, and as they struggled to open it they heard movement on the other side. Either they would die the moment they slid back the last bolt, or they would be heroes. With no time to waste worrying, they retracted the bolt. Treetop was thrown backward with such force against the wall behind them that he was knocked breathless. Long Flight and Breezer jumped aside, but only to feel strong arms press them to the wall and blades thrust against their throats.

The otters, their eyes not yet accustomed to the light, nearly killed the two Flyers before they recognized them. Trouter signalled with his paws to indicate silence while he winked and nodded thanks to the two young Flyers. He motioned for an otter to drag the unconscious Treetop into the storage room to recover. He whispered to Long Flight and Breezer to stay with their friend. The instant he awoke they were to retreat through the hole in the wall and report to One Eye. Pushing the two Flyers inside the storeroom, he re-bolted the door and motioned for the squad to advance.

Weapons drawn, they split into two halves, moving along each wall of the hallway. Trouter dispatched two otters to the ramparts as lookouts. The rest of them advanced to the noisy doorway. Pausing to take a few deep breaths, they burst into the room at full speed, firing sling stones.

The unsuspecting rats had no time to draw weapons before the otters were upon them. Some died with their paws still at their mouths, caught in the act of stuffing food into their yaps. Others at the far end of the room had time to look up, but only to expose their chests to a knife tip.

One rat, obviously an experienced fighter, managed to bring a weapon to bear upon the knife of Trouter. Jumping backward onto a table, the huge rat swung violently downward onto the otter's smaller blade, almost knocking it from his paw. Glimpsing a moment of opportunity to raise an alarm, the burly rat launched himself upward off the table and onto a stone windowsill.

Trouter regained his balance and leapt onto the wooden table, swinging wildly at the rat's legs with his knife. His only thought was to silence the rat before he signalled an alarm to the fortress.

The rat deflected Trouter's blow and viciously pushed the otter backward with a powerful kick to the chest. Using the seconds of time gained, he turned to the window's opening. The rat's piercing warning cry silenced the commotion in the room with a chilling certainty. They had been given away!

There could be no solace that the warning was cut short by Trouter's upward knife thrust. With the element of surprise removed, the battle plan lay in tatters.

‹›

Trouter could hear the alarm echo through the gigantic fortress, but they had to carry on; it was too late to turn back now. He dispatched fighters to the rooftop to lower the flag, the signal for Smidge and his troops to begin their assault.

Once the battle started, Trouter and his platoon were to provide covering fire for the attacking troops with slings and whatever else they could find. He sent a search party through the guard building to find bows, arrows, swords—anything useful for battle. Two slingers were placed at each window facing Magnath, and the rest were sent to the rooftop.

Grabbing a large knife and a sword from one of the victims, Trouter hurried up to the roof. Taking the stairs two at a time, he crested the top of the stairway, only to stop short in shock.

Three of his slingers were already dead with crossbow bolts protruding from their chests. He instinctively dove for cover, but not before a black shafted arrow whizzed by his ear, smashing loudly into the wall of stone behind him.

Earlier, the rats may have been asleep and complacent, but not now! He stole a brief look and immediately understood the strength of the enemy. The battle-hardened rats had quickly roused from their slumber and were pouring onto the ramparts of the fortress.

His inexperienced troops had not taken adequate cover and had been easily picked off by the king's expert crossbow archers. Now Trouter's surviving fighters were cowering, frightened out of their minds. How quickly they had experienced the ups and downs of war, from the exhilaration of early victory to absolute terror.

This was going to be a very long day indeed, thought Trouter, as he lay on his stomach, watching arrow after arrow rain down on them. Above him, the flag of Magnath seemed to taunt his troops as it snapped open, flying high in the morning breeze.

∾

Treetop began to moan softly as Long Flight and Breezer pulled him through the opening in the storage room wall into daylight.

"What happened? Am I dead?"

"No, you're not dead. You are just dead weight! Stand up and let's make a run for it!" Long Flight's tone was urgent.

The three young Flyers ran for the cover of the woods—the first heroes of the battle. Would they be the last? The warning from the guardhouse had awakened the evil of Magnath, and they could hear the otters' cries of suffering.

16

TERROR

Fortress Magnath

Smidge and the Manorwood troops slept for a few hours in the woods, camouflaged with leaves and pieces of bark. At first light, they moved forward to the forest edge to take up their positions and be ready to draw the enemy away from the main gate by firing arrows and slinging rocks at the top of the south wall.

They had been waiting for the flag on the guardhouse to come down, but Smidge and Mash watched in horror as the fortress walls came alive with the enemy. How had the surprise been lost? What should they do now? Smidge dispatched a Flyer to One Eye's headquarters for instructions. Paralyzed by the sight of the mighty beast of Magnath awaking, Mash stared in awe.

Smidge pushed him hard on the shoulder. "We've lost surprise but we haven't lost the battle. I have an idea."

The two friends knelt down and Mash looked on studiously as Smidge, using an arrow tip, drew out his plan in the dirt.

❧

One Eye digested the bad news delivered by the Flyers with a closed eye. He was deeply saddened to hear of the first loss of life amongst his troops. He knew he had to become accustomed to it, but these first deaths reminded him of how difficult and costly a victory was going to be.

Turning to Flyboy, he spoke urgently. "Send the Flyers out and call everyone back to the rally point for a new plan. Go with speed."

Turning to his maps, One Eye muttered to himself. "The rats are too strong. We must lure them out of the fortress somehow, or else they will simply slaughter us from the ramparts." Pointing to a spot on the map out of arrow range from the fortress, he continued, his voice stronger. "Pierre, after we regroup we will move eastward through the woods into the meadow and position ourselves here. We shall draw them out for a battle on our terms!"

Pierre turned toward the camp and shouted, "Get your weapons! Gather the reserves! Let's move!"

The entire camp burst into a frenzy of activity.

One Eye felt nauseated with anxiety; exactly how they would get the rats out of their impenetrable fortress he had no idea.

❧

Aswar surveyed the situation from the eastern wall. The few beasts holding the guardhouse were now pinned down by withering crossbow fire. Soon, there would also be stones hurling towards them from the light catapults now being moved into position. A smaller version of the enormous, ground-based, boulder-hurling weapons had been Jakbo's idea. Light enough to be moved to the top of the walls, the small catapults had proved invaluable. What they lost in the size of ammunition, they gained in manoeuvrability and accuracy. The enemy would soon know that smaller stones could carry a hefty wallop when tossed from the lofty walls of the fortress.

These few beasts would not be any kind of match for Magnath's experienced troops. Not often did anyone try to attack the fortress, but when they did it usually was more of a protest than a full-scale assault. When the stones and arrows started to fly from the high walls, the protesters hightailed it back into the forest. He could easily see the rest of this band of foolish attackers at the edge of the forest. Their inexperience was obvious. They were poorly hidden and were not in a recognizable battle formation. This would be an easy job.

Aswar dreaded the ensuing bloodshed, but if this "problem" were not dealt with quickly and forcibly, Magnath's anger would know no bounds. A job was a job. Aswar gave his commands briskly. The messenger ran down the stairs to the waiting soldiers.

☙

When stones were added to the deadly downpour of arrows upon the guardhouse roof, Trouter realized they must retreat. They were of no use pinned down on the rooftop. He shouted the order to withdraw and then cast one last look up at the fortress. He could see one beast dressed in black armour towering above the other rats. This must be Aswar, the heartless leader of the Magnath army. Trouter shuddered, quickly rose to his paws and ran for the stairway.

Out of breath from their retreat to the rendezvous point, Trouter's otters recovered and waited for everyone to arrive. Trouter had barely started reporting to One Eye when the Flyers sounded an alarm. With the view partially obscured by the guardhouse, no beast had seen the huge wooden gate of the dark, stone-cold fortress opening like a serpent's mouth. The column of black-armoured rats advancing outward broke into two separate prongs that looked like the forked tongue of a rattlesnake. The black rats, running at a terrifying speed, were almost at the forest edge. The scourge would be upon them in an instant!

One Eye had to make a quick decision. The rats had been drawn out of their fortress, but not on his terms. In horror, the squirrel leader watched the two pincers of the attack begin to envelop them. It was too late to run.

Standing tall, with his sword held high above his head, One Eye barked out commands from his position in the red oak tree. "Archers and slingers, prepare to fire on my word."

Ting responded with a terse, "Ready." The leaves of the surrounding trees shook as the squirrels loaded arrows and stones and adjusted their positions.

"Lancers form a line à moi, très fast. Swords behind dem," barked Pierre.

Because of their powerful shoulders, beavers were formidable lancers. When they planted their large, flat tails on the ground for support, it was impossible to knock them over. However, if they had to move, they were terribly slow on their paws.

With the rats almost upon them, the sword beasts barely had time to move into position. Otters could do many things, but the Farland otters were particularly skilled at sword- and knife-play. They formed groups of six, shoulder to shoulder. This way, if they had to they could easily form a tight circle, swords facing out, with their backs protected.

There was no time for further preparation. The rats were close enough that One Eye could hear the grunts of their laboured breathing. The centre of the rats' advance had been filled in with archers, who had taken a position in the field. From there, the larger bows of the rats could fling arrows at the Farlanders without worry that the squirrel's inferior bow shots could reach them.

Trouter braced himself for the onslaught. Drawing his knife in one paw and his sword in the other, he joined the closest otter formation. As he ran, he heard One Eye command the archers and slingers to fire at will. His words were lost in a deafening hiss as the first wave of enemy arrows ripped through the forest canopy.

Like autumn leaves, squirrels were falling to the ground, wounded or dead. The survivors returned fire as best they could. A few front-running rats were taken down with arrows in the paw or leg and others were knocked senseless by stones. However, like an unstoppable wave, the black mob swelled toward them.

Beaver lances lashed outward. The powerful beasts had enough strength to pierce the rats' chest armour, but their lances quickly became entangled. As the beavers paused to pull their weapons free, sword blows rained down on them. Wounded, surrounded and stripped of their lances, the beavers desperately swung their fists at the onrushing rats. The defensive line fell, and the rats encircled the Farlanders.

The otters, realizing they too would soon be surrounded, formed their circular defence, but as they did so a deadly shower of arrows hit them, striking rats and otters alike. Trouter could not believe that Magnath would fire into the midst of its own soldiers. At least ten otters fell to the ground instantly, dead or wounded, but so did an equal number of rats, arrows protruding from their backs. Rats swarmed around him. He dispatched one, but he had no time to react to the second, and he fell back with a deep wound in his leg.

Ting's troops had given up trying to reach the enemy archers and had turned their fire on the rats below. Their rate of fire had to slow, as they carefully selected their targets. The rats' front chest armour was too thick to penetrate, so they aimed for exposed body parts or the thinner back plate.

Ting exclaimed with satisfaction "Good, Good!" each time a rat was felled by his squad. Spotting a burly rat that had raised his sword, about to strike a wounded otter, the mighty little Woodland mouse expertly drew his bow. His arrow was aimed at the neck of the rat, but as he released his shot, he slumped forward and slowly cartwheeled to the ground, a black arrow in his chest.

Trouter, saved by Ting's last arrow, ran in retreat, painfully dragging his useless leg.

Aswar watched grimly as the feeble army of rebels was surrounded and about to be massacred by Magnath's soldiers.

⌘

Alex was suffering from exhaustion after the two-day journey to Magnath and had been ordered by Pierre to rest at camp for the morning so he could be of more help later in the day. Marta, not wanting to leave him, had volunteered to nurse the wounded. In preparation for emergencies, she had torn white cloth into strips for bandages and tucked these into her belt.

Totally unaware of the changing fortunes of their comrades, Alex and Marta had been idly chatting with the beasts held back to sharpen arrows, pick sling rocks and repair equipment. Their mood became increasingly anxious as the sounds of battle came closer and closer. Suddenly, several scared and wounded otters and squirrels stumbled into camp.

"Help me! I can't see!" cried one squirrel, whose vision was obscured by blood coming from a nasty wound on his scalp.

Marta calmed the poor creature and then expertly wrapped a bandage around his head, while he and the other survivors described the carnage and destruction on the battlefield. As Marta listened, she understood that it would get much worse if the rest of the trapped fighters could not escape. Running to her pack, she grabbed her uncle's massive sword. Turning, she surveyed the collection of beasts One Eye had considered too young or too old to join the attack.

"Gather up any weapons you can find. We must open a retreat passage for our friends. Hurry!" The group needed no further encouragement. Alex was overjoyed to finally feel useful. Minutes later, the motley crew followed Marta into the woods toward the sounds of the battle.

Within a hundred metres of their camp, Marta sighted black rats attacking a group of otters from all sides. Gesturing urgently for her "soldiers" to spread out to the left and right, she raised her sword and charged forward, screaming, "Death to Magnath!"

The intense and unexpected attack from Marta's warriors bewildered the rats, who had thought the battle was already won.

Marta jumped from log to log, insanely swinging her sword from side to side and delivering punishing blows. Squirrels fired arrows as fast as they could, and Alex's sling stones found their mark more often than not. The rest of the group worked in clusters of three and four to confront rats separated from the main attack and force them away from the beleaguered otters.

A young otter stumbled toward Marta, bleeding profusely from a leg wound. A sword-wielding rat charged forward in hot pursuit. Recognizing Trouter from the hockey game, she called for him to duck. With a running jump, she sailed over the Farlander and plunged her sword through the black chest armour of the pursuer. Weakly, Trouter fell to the ground. Marta rushed over and swiftly pulled a bandage from her belt to apply as a tourniquet.

"Well, Marta, I never thought I'd be so glad to see you and your apron as I am right now. Thanks."

"No problem. We're all in this together."

Helping the beast to his paws, she saw that her troops had immobilized at least twenty rats and had opened a clear path of retreat. Yelling as loudly as she could, Marta signalled the Farlanders. One Eye and Pierre twisted their heads away from the battle long enough to see Marta signalling wildly with her arms, indicating a clear passage back to camp.

"Retreat! Retreat!" shouted the leaders in raspy unison.

Pierre was so scared he could barely get the word "retreat" out of his dry throat. The thought of withdrawal caused hot tears of anger to flow down his dusty face, but he turned and ran. He would have been surprised to know that the rats were relieved to see them leave.

The battle had been more vicious than they had expected, and they were eager to return to the safety of their fortress.

❦

Smidge's plan had been to create a catapult powerful enough to launch a large stone all the way to the main gate of the fortress. To test his idea, he had bent over six ash saplings. Then, with Pete lying on the treetops to weigh them down, he lashed the trees together with vines. Unfortunately, Broadtail, whose arms ached from pinning down the treetops, loosened his grip. With a scream of terror, Pete became airborne and was hurled about ten metres away. As he hit the ground, a large whoomp of air escaped from his chest.

"You eeee-deee-ots! You could have got me killed. I think every bone in my body is broken!" wailed the groundhog.

"Well, your mouth is still working," laughed Mash and Grunch.

"And we know the catapult works! Now let's get to work," added Smidge excitedly. "Everyone, start gathering stones!"

After Pete received an apology and extra rations to eat, he agreed to bend over groups of four saplings—but only four. Once they were secured, a basket of branches was tied crossways near the treetops to hold a rock. A single rope fixed the top of the catapult to the ground. One sword blow to the rope would send the rock hurling toward Magnath. After a frenzy of activity, the entire ash grove disappeared, and dozens of makeshift weapons emerged in its place.

Mash, Smidge and Pete were standing back to admire their work when a Flyer squirrel touched down near them. Before she could catch her breath, she urgently announced, "One Eye orders you to hold your attack and wait for further orders."

The friends looked at each other in frustration, but knew that an order was an order.

"Let's take the stones off so the trees don't lose their spring. Don't worry. We'll have our time," said Smidge bravely.

One Eye had abandoned his command tree and had joined the retreating troops heading toward camp. Their pace had slowed to a stumble as the exhausted fighters realized that the rats were not giving chase. Many of the survivors were wounded, and most had dropped their weapons in their eagerness to escape. It was most discouraging to see their eyes full of wild fear and their faces expressionless, like wooden masks.

The moment One Eye entered camp, he barked out orders.

"Start the fires. We need hot water to tend to the wounded, and everyone needs a meal."

One of the young ones, obviously worried, questioned One Eye. "But the rats will see the smoke."

"It doesn't matter anymore. There is no surprise now. Has anyone seen General Lech yet?"

"I think he has just arrived, sir."

"Go tell him when he is rested to come and see me at my campsite. I need his counsel." Turning to help some of the wounded to the hospital

area, he yelled at a group of young mice who were standing together, paralyzed with fear. "Go gather all the arrows and weapons you can find on the battlefield. This isn't over yet."

The young mice first looked at each other with skepticism and then nodded consent, their faces set with grim determination.

*

Jakbo stood beside Aswar and supervised the return of the victorious rats, patting them on the shoulder for a job well done as they re-entered the fortress gate. The soldiers were grinning and laughing, knowing that as a reward tonight they would receive extra food and drink.

Aswar dispatched new sentries to the guardhouse to ensure all the attackers were gone and to re-establish the lookout. Then he ordered the monstrous wooden gate closed and locked.

Relieved, he headed up the stairs two at a time to take a final look at the surrounding forest before he reported to the king. Seeing nothing but the remains of the fallen, he turned and then stopped to think. Had he not seen among them squirrels, otters, beavers and mice? It was unusual that there were so many different beasts attacking. Normally, one group or another made a feeble attempt to overthrow the king. Who dared to lead this attack?

*

After receiving detailed reports of the heavy losses among his troops, One Eye was having second thoughts about continuing the attack. He wiped tears from his eye. "I can't believe Ting, my dear friend, is dead. I lost so many good soldiers today."

Trying to console the distraught squirrel, Pierre patted him on the shoulder. "Trouter tells me Ting saved his life. Your friend died bravely in battle."

One Eye bowed his head. "My plan failed. It's my fault, and the best thing to do is forget the whole stupid idea and go home."

General Lech had listened intently to every detail of the battle and subsequent defeat. Closing his eyes, he thoughtfully stroked his grey whiskers. Pierre, Flyboy, Gerr and One Eye all waited patiently, holding what were now empty food plates in their paws. After a long silence, the General finally spoke softly, but strongly.

"Any battle worth winning is never won easily. Leaving now would dishonour Ting and our other friends who have already perished for our cause. It is a worthy goal to free the forests of the great oppressor, Magnath. It is not a stupid idea." Then, he added more emphatically, "But we will never conquer the walls of that fortress."

The group hung their heads in despair.

"I thought we weren't going to give up!" Flyboy said angrily.

Obviously irritated that he had been interrupted, Lech raised his voice for the first time. "Silence, son, and listen. We must use our defeat today to our advantage. If we can't breach the walls, then cunning, deception and patience will lead our way to victory. Now, pay attention."

The leaders gathered in closely to hear every word the old warrior spoke. By the time Lech was finished, everyone had a thorough understanding of the plan and his responsibilities.

One Eye broke the ensuing silence. "Pierre, get four or five beavers here to start sharpening poles. Flyboy and Gerr, find every available mole to dig."

"Okay, beasts, we start work the instant it is dark," added Pierre.

❧

Wanting to be alone, Smidge had wandered away from the rest of the Manorwood beasts. He had been so hopeful. Now, the dream of being with his father seemed unattainable. There was no way they were going to get inside that massive fortress to free anyone. He slumped despondently against a log and closed his eyes.

Without warning, a heavy paw seized his shoulder. His heart leapt into his mouth with fear. Obviously, the black rats had outflanked them! He was preparing himself for the worst when a low voice spoke.

"I thought I told you not to do this."

That voice! "Duke, is that you?" He twisted sharply, and the grip of the huge paw loosened. The two friends heartily embraced.

"What are you doing here?"

"Well, after you left, I got to thinking. I've been wasting my life, wallowing in self-pity all alone out there in the woods, and I hadn't had a friend in a long time, until you. So, if I can't get my dear wife back, maybe I can help a friend get his father back. Here I am, laddie—Duke, the Black Rat Slayer, at your service."

With a jaunty salute, he started marching toward the rest of the Manorwood Brigade, with Smidge jogging behind. Mash and Pete couldn't believe their eyes when they saw the massive rabbit lumber out of the bushes. After a round of greetings, Duke listened intently to the day's events up until then.

"Our surprise has been lost. We don't know what happened. We were just told to wait, but from the sounds we heard, there must already have been a battle," reported Mash.

"Yeah, and we had just got our groundhog-tossing catapults ready for action." Smidge winked at Pete while pointing to their freshly made weapons.

"Well, they won't be too effective, will they, if you only have one groundhog to toss!" chortled Duke.

"Oh no, I'll just run back as fast as I can, and they can load me up again," replied Pete.

Now, everyone broke into laughter and the gloom that had lain so heavily over the camp began to lift.

Duke rose to his hind paws and surveyed the troops. "Lads, we will have our moment, so let's be prepared. The last time I was here, I watched as the rats dragged my dear wife Violet into that evil toilet-hole of a fort. That was long ago, and there is no saving her now, but I will bring down that evil king and find Smidge's father if it's the last thing I do! Are ye with me?"

Quiet cheers rose upward into the trees, from everyone except Smidge, who with his face in his paws had begun to cry uncontrollably, overcome by the show of support from his friends.

"Now, lads, when I was here, those many eons ago, I hid behind an outstanding pile of rocks. I think they will be exceptionally useful to smash forts and flatten rats! Let's go get some!" With spring in his gait, Duke led a rejuvenated band of warriors into the woods to gather ammunition.

Smidge wiped away his tears and followed, quickly catching up to Pete and delivering a solid body check.

"Hurry up, Dirt Digger, you're in my way!" he teased.

"Don't worry, River Rat, I am moving as fast as I can, because the more rocks we get, the lower the chance I'll get catapulted."

ᏇᎧ

Teams of mice and groundhogs hauled dirt piled onto blankets out of an enlarging tunnel. Every movement was performed as silently as possible, so as not to alert the guards of Magnath. The beasts worked in shifts while tired workers rested by the stream. After soaking their weary paws and eating, they returned immediately to the task.

One Eye looked on with a watchful gaze, nervously pacing back and forth. It soon would be dawn and time to execute the plan. Victory or total annihilation hinged on the choices he and the other leaders made, but he had been the one who had made the final decision to proceed with the old squirrel's proposal. He had displayed confidence so the others would believe the bold idea would work—that was leadership. Being a good leader also meant being prepared, so once again, he went to check on the readiness of the troops who would carry out the plan, risking their lives in the process. Off he went to pace, to worry and to spend a sleepless night.

ↄ

A Flyer messenger had arrived in the middle of the night to advise the Manorwood Brigade of the new plans. The message was simple: to be ready at dawn to do whatever they could to help. The otters and squirrels, tired from hours of carrying rocks, traded bewildered looks when they received the vague instructions. Smidge reassured them that they had enough rocks to cause serious destruction and told them not to worry. But before he finished his pep talk, most of the beasts were sound asleep.

As dawn approached, One Eye watched as the final preparations were carried out. The tunnel entrance was filled with dirt and rocks. Their work completed, the diggers trudged wearily to the stream to bathe away dirt from the night's work. Around them, anxious warriors rose to complete their pre-battle rituals. Swords were sharpened, arrows tipped and lances cut.

"Are you ready, Pierre? Flyboy? Gerr?" asked One Eye, looking each one of them briefly in the eye.

Each nodded in turn, and as they left, the exhausted leader bade them good luck.

17

ATTACK OF THE MANORWOOD BRIGADE

Fortress Magnath

Aswar could not believe the foolishness of these beasts. The edge of the forest once again brimmed with telltale signs of their presence. Leaves and branches stirred unnaturally, unlike any wind-created movement. Occasional glints of light reflecting off steel in the early morning sun were like beacons to his well-trained eye. He had been roused from his bed by the astonished sentries. Clearly, he had been hasty last night when he had reported to the king that the enemy was vanquished. The job must be done this time, or he, himself, would be doomed.

In the corridor, Jakbo, who was rushing to attend the king, greeted him with a menacing scowl. "This morning should be good blood sport for the troops." Then, stopping on his way past, he tapped Aswar emphatically on his chest armour. "Take no prisoners. Do the king proud, or you will be on the next slave ship." A wicked smile flashed across his face as he turned and hurried on his way.

❧

Gerr sat with his troops on the damp ground behind some spruce trees and looked down the battle line toward its far end, where Pierre and his fighters were hidden. He smiled. The attack force was as prepared as it could be.

On command, the mice, voles and moles along the forest edge began shaking branches and flashing their knives in the sunlight. Patiently, they waited for the rats to make their move.

Some of the mud spread on his face for camouflage had dried, and pieces fell to the ground as Gerr's smile widened with anticipation. What a surprise those arrogant rodents were about to receive.

❧

Aswar marched along the rampart, flanked by his commanders, looking carefully at the terrain surrounding the fortress. There did not appear to be any attackers other than those lurking along the forest edge. "I shall personally lead the troops on the ground."

"Don't you think that is dangerous, sir?" questioned his surprised captain.

"Not at all. Clearly, we are dealing with amateurs here. Let's move."

Aswar adjusted his ornate face shield, unsheathed his sword and briskly marched toward the stairs. Taking the steps two at a time, he emerged onto the main grounds of the fortress. Before him was an impressive sight: row upon row of rats in rank and file with their shields up and lances forward. Behind the lancers were the sword beasts, and at the rear were the short-bow archers. The long-bow archers stood assembled on the walls above.

Aswar assumed his position with the sword beasts. Slowly he raised his arm, his fearsome sword catching sun and reflecting a shard of light across the cobblestones below. After one last look along his lines of troops, he nodded for the gatekeepers to haul the ropes that opened the front gate. He took an enormous breath, then swung his arm down as he yelled, "Magnath!"

Raising a blinding cloud of dust, the swarm of black-armoured rats charged out the fortress' stony throat and across the field toward the forest's edge. The clanking of armour and swords shattered the early morning silence. Arrows from the archers on the fortress walls flew over the helmets of the onrushing rats, whizzing into the foliage at the edge of the forest.

Gerr cringed at the sound of the deadly deluge and the shaking of the earth caused by the hundreds of heavy paws charging toward them.

Pierre whispered, "Mon Dieu," and dropped even lower in his hiding spot as the rats' tremendous firepower rained upon them.

Alex and Marta stood shoulder-to-shoulder with Trouter and the rest of the otters and squirrels of the reserve attack force, hidden farther back in the woods. Trouter, his agility impaired by his heavily bandaged leg, had traded his sword for a bow and arrow. Alex brandished a battered but very large blade that he had recovered from the battlefield. Marta rested her uncle's magnificent sword upon her shoulder. They waited for the signal to move.

One Eye watched from his post in the red oak tree, his vision obscured by the dust cloud wafting slowly toward him with the light morning breeze. Below him he could see the mice and moles already retreating from the forest's edge. Many were bleeding from wounds, and those left behind lay motionless on the forest floor, impaled by arrows. They had done their job as decoys with great bravery. The rats, seeing the rebel force retreat, charged even harder toward the edge of the forest.

At each end of the line, there was no movement from either Pierre's or Gerr's troops.

Suddenly, just as the wave of rat lancers approached the forest's edge, an ear-shattering eruption of noise rose into the air—the sound of heavily armoured rats crashing into each other. This was quickly followed by cries of surprise as the rodents plummeted into the deep tunnel that had been dug by the moles and groundhogs. When the thin roof of dirt and grass concealing the long pit gave way, a huge plume of dust shot straight upward into the air. The sharpened stakes at the bottom of the void provided a most unpleasant landing area for the victims as they piled on top of each other. Many of the rats in the second wave could not break their momentum in time before they too slipped over the edge. Others could not see the deadly trap in the dust and confusion of battle and ran full-speed into their painful demise.

Seeing what had happened to the beasts just ahead of him, Aswar cursed under his breath. Behind the mask, his face flushed deeply with anger at being tricked. Quickly assessing the situation, he knew what was coming next. The two pincers of the rebel army, led by Gerr and Pierre, burst from the forest. Their battle cries drowned out the screams of the rats. Before Aswar could raise his voice to command his remaining troops to halt, a deadly hail of large stones hurled down upon the unsuspecting black horde. The deadly missiles plowed into the soldiers to the left and right of Aswar, killing them instantly or injuring them badly enough to make them useless. Some larger stones hit the fortress with such force that the thinner walls on top of the main buttress collapsed, silencing many of the longbow archers.

One Eye's tired face smiled, enjoying a brief moment of satisfaction. He could see the army of Magnath in disarray on the far side of the pit. The barrage from Smidge and the Manorwood Brigade had wreaked more damage than he could have dreamt. Unable to move forward, the dazed rats just stood still, waiting for direction. Eager to avenge Ting's death, the archers opened fire with all the strength they could muster, launching arrows from the trees as fast as their paws would allow. Completely disoriented by the rapid turn of events, hundreds of rats started running back toward the fortress. Feeling almost calm, One Eye motioned to Flyboy to release the second part of the plan.

Aswar screamed at the deserters to maintain their formation and prepare to repel the assault from each side. But he was surprised to see that the attackers were not wasting time engaging his soldiers and were instead rushing full tilt toward the main gate. He knew his gatekeepers would shut the gate once they saw the rebels nearing the entrance to the fortress, which would trap him and his troops outside.

"Retreat!" Aswar shouted, as he turned and ran, pushing his stumbling and confused soldiers ahead of him. The battle had become a deadly race to control the entrance to the fortress.

With the go-ahead from One Eye, the Flyers knew it was time for them to enter the battle. They had to seize control of the gate. Once Pierre's and Gerr's troops were inside the fortress, the Flyers would drop the gate to prevent the rats from following. There could be no failure, or all would be lost.

Loaded with ammunition, the younger Flyers were anxious to launch the attack on the gatehouse. With Flyboy's arrival, they completed a final check of their flight suits. Treetop, Long Flight and Breezer looked each other in the eye one last time, nodded and then pushed off with all their might into the rising wind. Stretching their limbs as far as they could to capture all the wind power available, they hurled themselves toward the chaos of the battle. Behind them, twenty other Flyers, led by Flyboy, formed a triangular flight formation, the point directed at the main gate of the fortress.

As hoped for, the silent passage of the first three Flyers over the north bastions went unnoticed, and Treetop and Long Flight landed just inside the wall nearest the door of the gatehouse. But Breezer, always bold, stayed airborne to find a target for his stones, alerting the guards on the north wall. Unfortunately, his zeal cost him his life, as a hail of arrows sent him crashing to the ground. While Flyboy's flight group attracted a barrage of missiles, the two Flyers on the ground went unnoticed in the confusion. The diversion was short-lived. As Long Flight reached for the door handle, the cries of a dozen rats rang out around them.

"Enemy inside! Get them!" A burly rat armed with a broadsword charged toward Treetop. When he raised his weapon to strike the inadequately armed squirrel, a rock struck him and he lurched forward, falling limply to the ground. Treetop snatched a knife from the belt of the fallen rat.

A hail of bombs from Flyboy and the other Flyers crashed down upon the remaining rats. Bodies and rocks fell to the ground as Treetop and Long Flight burst into the gatehouse.

Two muscular rats were working the large rope used to lower the heavy gate. One rat dropped the rope, grabbed a nearby sword and charged at Treetop. Thinking that the squirrels had come through the main entrance, the second rat desperately

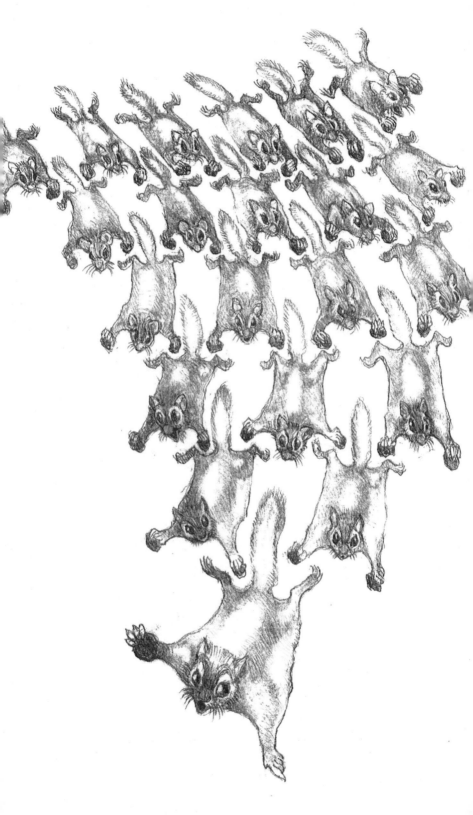

continued to lower the gate to prevent more intruders from entering. Treetop's weapon was no match for the rat's sword, and his attacker's first powerful blow knocked the small knife from his paw, sending it clattering across the stone floor. Treetop dodged the following parry, but the next caught him in the shoulder. The searing pain made him collapse to the ground, clutching a gaping wound.

Just as the rat raised his sword for the final blow, his eyes widened with shock, and he dropped his weapon. He fell face first on the floor, clasping his paws around a knife protruding from his chest. Long Flight's accurate throw had saved his friend's life. However, precious time was being wasted as the other rat furiously hauled on the rope to close the gate.

Long Flight stood face-to-face with the rat, who was the remaining obstacle to control of the gate.

ᨪ

The Farland soldiers raced for the entrance, striking down any enemy they encountered. Pierre's and Gerr's squads were closing the pincers of the attack. Their soldiers moved into formation for the final push to the gate, but it was closing too soon—they had to get there first!

As the Farlanders and rats rushed toward the entrance, the long archers from the top of the wall fired frantically at the attackers. Their small catapults tossed rocks into the crowded battlefield with sickening effect. Bravely, the Farlanders fought paw-to-paw, inflicting casualties. But soon their rapid advance stalled as losses mounted. The otters, beavers and squirrels, with poor or no armour, were easy targets for the rat archers. Even worse, Aswar's lance beasts were pushing through the bedlam to form a passageway that would allow his troops to retreat into the fortress.

೧

Mash and Smidge urged the Manorwood troops to move more quickly. Pete and Duke ran from catapult to catapult, throwing themselves upon the treetops to bend them back. Breathlessly waiting for the securing rope to be tied, they then dashed off to the next machine. The moment they were off the catapult, the otters hoisted a large rock into the basket. A swift sword swing cut the tether rope and sent the projectile hurling toward Magnath.

Smidge had turned from the whirlwind of activity to scout out the best targets. The gate was closing! He could see rats turning and running under the partially closed gate. There was no time to waste. Once inside, the rats could easily fend off the attack from behind Magnath's walls. Instead of waiting for all the weapons to be reloaded, he ordered a salvo at the main gate. Maybe they could cause enough damage to prevent it from closing. "Fire! Fire!" he screamed, jumping up and down and pounding his paw on his thigh for emphasis.

೧

One Eye could see the lance rats forming an escape route. If they fled inside the fortress and closed the gate the battle would be lost in the next few moments. Lifting his sword, he dropped from his treetop perch to lead a new charge toward the fortress with the reserve battle force. The rest of the Farland army followed, screaming at the top of their lungs. Marta, Alex, Stride and Flash ran shoulder-to-shoulder toward the rats with their swords held high. Trouter, limping badly, followed close behind. Hearing the crash of the underbrush as the reinforcements charged out of the forest, Gerr and Pierre rallied the remainder of their soldiers to join the charge.

As the Farlanders approached the gate, they encountered a fierce-looking row of rat lance beasts prepared to stand their ground. Urged forward by One Eye, the two armies met with an ear-splitting clash of swords and shields. Pierre planted his tail and started wielding his pike. With mighty blows, he cleared a swath through the smaller enemy. Trouter fired arrows with great accuracy, running as fast as his wounded leg would allow. The metallic ring of sword upon sword filled the air, as did the whiz of arrows flying overhead to their deadly destinations. Marta and Alex worked as a team with their swords, one striking low and the other high. Marta, in the confusion, worried she would kill a Farlander. The dust and noise was overwhelming, but when her resolve started to drain, to see the ferocity of her little brother's attack allowed her heart to regain the strength to carry on.

The tide of the battle was changing in favour of the Farlanders, but many of the rats were retreating through the slowly descending gate. Over the bedlam of the battle the thunderous sound of the stones hitting the gate's tower was deafening. Plumes of dust and debris soared into the air as rocks pounded the ancient stonework of the fortress. Inside the gatehouse, Long Flight and Treetop watched as dust and pieces of stone from the collapsing ceiling showered the rat lowering the gate. With arm-wrenching suddenness, the rope jerked to a halt and the rat stumbled off balance.

Long Flight seized the moment. Quickly moving forward, he dispatched the floundering rat with Treetop's knife. Grabbing the rope, he pulled down with his entire weight. The gate was inoperable! He gave one last pull on the rope, to no avail, then ran to the small window overlooking the entrance to the fortress. The damaged gate remained stuck with an opening just high enough above ground to allow the enemy to crawl underneath it. The rats were pushing and struggling with each other, trying to wiggle under the gate.

Aswar had already escaped inside and was calling for his remaining warriors to follow. His futile command for the gate to be closed could barely be heard above the din of the battle.

Long Flight watched from the small window above and smiled. Despite the fact that his mission was not going according to plan, not all had been lost. With the gate immovable, at least the rats could not stop the Farlanders from entering the fortress as well.

❧

Duke could see the flow of the battle change after the last barrage of rocks. The gate was no longer moving, but the rats and Farlanders were locked in a fight for control of the entrance.

"Well, lads and lassies, it is time for us to join the fray. Gather your weapons and let's go, because the real party is about to begin!" Smidge, Mash, Grunch and Pete joined in behind the large rabbit as he bounded toward the fortress gate.

Smidge lifted his sword over his head and screamed, "Manorwood Brigade—attack!"

The rest of the beasts, hearing the heart-felt yell, joined in, and soon it became their war cry as they chanted it all the way to the battle.

As the Manorwood Brigade approached the fray, they could see Farlanders struggling against the powerful rats. Undeterred, the brigade members joined the battle. Fearlessly, Broadtail led the charge, but stumbled and fell when he became the victim of a crossbow.

The loss of their comrade only strengthened the others' resolve, and they threw themselves into the midst of the struggle for the gate. Arms whirling, Flash slung stones like a mad beast. Beside her, Stride swung Gerr's small sword with strength he never knew he possessed.

Noticing the ferocity of Stride's charge, Gerr moved toward the young otter, blocking blow after blow from rat lances. Never breaking the rhythm of his sword, Gerr grunted out of the side of his mouth, "Stride, I am glad to see all that practice with my sword is paying off. You can keep it. You've earned it." After deftly side-stepping a lance, he lunged toward the assailant. Then, the battle lines blurred and Gerr disappeared into the mayhem.

Smidge and Mash rushed toward Marta and Alex, but there was no time for greetings as arrows whipped overhead. Marta had time for a brief smile at Mash before an injured rat suddenly recovered enough strength to stand up and run for the gate. Alex stuck out his paw to trip the rat, and Marta dispatched the beast with a quick sword thrust. With admiration in his eyes, Mash returned her smile with a wink and a grin.

"Marauder!"

The four of them resumed their progress toward the gateway. They were all surprised to see Duke and Pete ahead of them, bravely dodging arrows and climbing over the wounded to grab hold of the heavy wooden gate. They strained to raise it enough to allow their comrades to run under instead of crawl.

Duke peered under the gate and could see disaster looming if enough Farlanders couldn't get through the opening immediately. The rats were lining up three deep in the courtyard under the command of their masked leader. They must seize the moment before the rats counterattacked. Looking back toward Gerr and Pierre, he urgently signalled every beast still able to fight to move forward. Then, the huge rabbit squeezed under the gate as Pete created just enough space with a final powerful heave upward.

Once inside, Duke ran at full speed directly toward the rats' formation. Reaching the first enemy line, he twisted, jumped, stretched out horizontally, hurled himself at the rats and knocked at least fifteen off their paws. The sheer boldness of his singular attack destroyed the rats' confidence and they started to break formation.

The rest of the Farlanders rushed under the gate.

"Well done, Pete! You got us in!" Smidge shouted as he ran by, patting his friend on the shoulder.

"At least there wasn't a moat to swim," muttered the groundhog, his arms trembling with exertion.

Aswar, standing off to the side of the courtyard, could see the Farlanders entering the fortress en masse. He was about to command his troops to hold the line when a rocketing arrow from Trouter's bow struck him in the shoulder. The impact twisted him around, and he fell backwards into a doorway.

From where he lay, he could see the rats' king standing in the window of his chamber. He looked very frightened as he urgently gestured for Aswar to rise and launch a counterattack against the rebels. Aswar smiled and lay down his head. Welcoming the pain that radiated outward from the wound, he made no attempt to stop the loss of blood. He was finished obeying that crazy ogre.

"Attack!" screamed Smidge, joining the voices of the brigade and the Farlanders.

They raced across the courtyard, meeting very little resistance, as most of the rats had realized the battle was lost. The leaderless hoard only wanted to escape as fast as it could run. Smidge and Flash whipped sling stones at anything that moved.

When they had last seen Duke, he had been frenzied— twirling and twisting, flattening or killing as many rats as he possibly could. When they fought across the courtyard, they found the huge beast sitting on the cobblestones, breathing heavily. He did not look well. Smidge rushed forward, extending an arm for support as his friend started to fall to one side.

"What's wrong?"

"Well, laddie, I think vengeance is rather sweet after all. But, unfortunately, it comes with a wee bit of a cost."

As the large beast leaned heavily against him, Smidge could see a large wound in the rabbit's flank that looked very deep.

"Oh, no, Duke, you'll be alright. We'll get the healers to fix you up."

"It's too late. 'Tis no matter. My dear Violet is long gone. But what will make all this worth the while is for you to find your father. Now get goin'!" With those last words, Duke slumped to one side and closed his eyes. Smidge held his friend in his arms and cried.

&

One Eye's voice rose above the conflict. "Gerr, Grunch, Trouter, Pierre, follow me to the king's court. We'll make sure that bully never takes another slave! Smidge, Mash, Pete, Marta and Alex, go to the prisoners' compound and the dungeons. Set them all free."

Smidge had already left.

18

THE DUNGEONS
OF MAGNATH

Fortress Magnath

When the prisoners realized the guards had abandoned their posts, they started pushing against the gate of their compound, trying to loosen the latch. Jagged rock shards protruding from the top of the high wall stopped some of the younger and fitter beasts as they attempted to climb over the barriers. Smidge arrived at the entrance first and lifted the two heavy logs used to lock the gate. The force of the slaves pushing against it suddenly met no resistance, and the heavy wooden structure swung open so quickly that the beasts closest to it pitched forward and hit the ground. The fallen were nearly trampled to death by the ensuing stampede. While screaming with joy for their freedom, some stopped briefly to hug their liberators before they rushed to scrounge for food, eager to gorge.

Marta and Alex helped some of the more frail beasts rise to their paws. Excitedly, Smidge and Pete hurried into the enclosure, stopping to ask a few of the stragglers if they had known an otter named Terramboe. None had. As the two walked further, they were overcome with sadness at the poor condition of some of the captives. Dirty and thin, they barely had the strength to walk toward the gate.

A deep rage filled Smidge's heart when he saw what the evil King Magnath had done to these beasts. His paws clenched and unclenched as he was overcome by anxiety about the condition in which he might find his father—or if he would find him at all. Stopping an older beast, who appeared to have been in the compound for many seasons, Smidge asked hopefully, "Sorry to bother you, sir, but have you met a big, tall otter named Terramboe?"

The poor old squirrel swayed rather than stood, and could barely find the strength to speak. "Sorry, son, but I haven't. Do you have any food?"

Smidge gave him a biscuit from his pouch. The poor beast ate it quickly. Wiping his lips with the back of his paw, he smiled, whispered, "Thank you," before shuffling off toward his freedom.

Smidge felt angry, desperate and very sad all at the same time. There was no way his father had survived. His energy suddenly drained from him, and he leaned against a wall.

Pete came up beside his friend and placed a huge digging paw on his shoulder. "You know, I think your father is so strong and dangerous, the only place that would hold him would be the dungeon. So, let's go check it out. Come on!"

Along with those encouraging words, Pete gave Smidge a friendly shove and, accompanied by Marta and Alex, they headed off toward a large, timbered door with a guard post on either side. Picking up the keys from one of the huts, they pushed open the heavily reinforced door. The dank smell of wet stone filled their nostrils as they descended the cool, slippery steps to the cells. The darkness was complete, except for a small amount of light filtering through narrow slits in the very top of the outer wall. Using the crudely made metal keys, they unlocked the cell doors one by one.

The prisoners barely stopped to say thank you as they rushed toward fresh air and daylight. In one cell sat an ancient-looking squirrel, his face distorted by a large scar running from below his left eye to the corner of his mouth. Slumped against the far wall of his dirty enclosure, he did not move, even when the door swung open. *This beast has been here a long time*, thought Smidge. *He might have heard of my father.*

"Sir, you are free to go," Smidge said brightly.

"Sir? Haven't heard that in a long time," rasped the old creature in a low voice. Chuckling to himself, he continued, "Free—free to go where? I have been in this cell so long that it has become my home. I have no friends or family left."

Smidge approached slowly and stopped halfway into the cell, overpowered by the stench of the unwashed beast. "Why were you held prisoner?"

"Magnath felt it was a punishment more cruel to rot in this cell than be executed." The squirrel dropped his head to his sunken chest. "He was right."

"What was your crime?"

"I led an attack on the fortress to try to end the evil, once and for all. As you see, we failed miserably."

"In all your time here, have you ever seen an otter named Terramboe?"

"No beast by such a name has been a prisoner here, son."

Tears of frustration began to fill his eyes, and Smidge could barely speak. Regaining self-control, he smiled and approached the decrepit prisoner. Despite his revulsion over the disgusting odour, he moved closer, feeling a strong bond with this old warrior—a beast brave enough to attack Magnath. "What is your name?"

"I was called Bolt, but nothing that polite for a long time."

"Well, Bolt, you deserve a warm bath and a good meal. Let me help you up."

Bolt, Smidge, Pete, Marta, Alex and Mash climbed the rough stone stairs out into the daylight. They had to stop frequently to allow Bolt to rest and permit his eyes to adjust to the light. As they passed into the main courtyard, they could see waves of attacking Farlanders rushing up the stairs into the palace. The courtyard was now a grim reminder of the battle that had been fought. Bodies lay strewn across the cool, grey cobblestones. Spent rocks, arrows and swords were scattered upon the ground. The weapons, no longer wielded in anger, seemed smaller, quiet, but the blood that soiled them spoke of the pain and suffering they had inflicted.

By the time they reached the palace, the skirmish had quieted, and Smidge led the way up the grand steps of the rat king's palatial lair. They were awestruck by the riches covering the walls. The king's grandiose display of loot gave the outer rooms the appearance of a huge trophy case.

Bolt, breathing deeply from his laborious journey up the stairs to Magnath's chambers, noticed the enthralled looks upon the friends' faces. "This is nothing, I hear the king's bed is gold and silver and the size of a small house!"

When they entered the king's quarters, they saw a majestic-looking figure, who could only be the queen, standing rigidly at the foot of an ornate bed. Despite the presence of warriors with swords, she seemed remarkably calm.

One Eye appeared furious as he waved his sword at the queen's jewel-covered neck. "One last time. Where is your husband, the so-called 'King'?"

"I told you, the second he saw the battle was lost, he and the captain of the guard ran like the cowards they are, leaving me here, defenceless." Almost screaming her last words, she fell backward onto the bed and began to sob.

Smidge edged toward the queen and knelt beside the bed. "Ma'am, did you ever meet an otter named Terramboe?"

The queen immediately stopped her weeping and gave Smidge a long, strange look. "Yes, I knew him well."

Smidge's heart leapt into his mouth. Finally, the first encouraging words of the entire quest! "Where is he?"

"He's dead," murmured the queen, turning her head to bury her face once again in the pillow.

"No! He can't be." Exhausted, Smidge could not restrain himself, and he burst into tears.

Pete and Mash moved to comfort him as his shoulders heaved with sobs.

The queen again turned her head and stared intensely at the anguished young otter. She raised herself on the pillow and spoke tenderly.

"I was very fond of Terramboe. He was a good beast and served our kingdom well." She paused and then continued. "You will find his body in the barracks on the far side of the courtyard."

"Served your kingdom! Yes, but as a slave!" Gerr's voice pinched tight with anger.

Smidge felt overwhelmed by shock and sadness, but he needed to see his father, even if all he could see was his dead body. Without hesitation, he dashed from the room down the stone stairs with reckless abandon.

His friends chased after him, only to be stopped at the doorway by One Eye's sword, barring the way. "He needs to do this alone. Let him be."

⁌

Breathlessly dodging bands of Farlanders searching for remaining rats, Smidge raced across the courtyard and entered the barracks' door. He called out his father's name. Moving farther inside, the only beast he could see was an enormous rat, dressed in full armour and lying motionless on the dirt floor. Recognizing Aswar's face shield and helmet, Smidge drew his sword and prodded the beast's paw.

"Looking for Terramboe?"

Jumping back with fright, Smidge recovered enough to answer. "Yes, he is my father. Where is he?"

"I am Terramboe, and you must be my son."

Smidge looked in disbelief at the rat, "You murderous liar! I don't believe a word you say, you scum."

"How are things in Manorwood, Smidge?"

"Anyone could know where I live! You can't be my father!"

" . . . and your mother, Silk?"

Smidge was confused. He stood silently, staring at the rat.

"How's the high toss going with the juggling sticks I made you?" As he spoke, he pushed up the mask that had disguised his otter features from those outside the walls of Magnath for many, many seasons.

Smidge's face slowly transformed from outrage and anger to shock and disbelief. "An otter! Why are you dressed up like a rat? I don't understand."

"I know I have much explaining to do. But you'd better take me prisoner before some beast tries to kill me."

Maybe he was being tricked! It had been so long since he had seen his father. How would he recognize him? Smidge couldn't take another moment without knowing. "I think you'd best tell me your story right now," said Smidge tersely, his sword ready.

The larger otter removed his helmet and put pressure on his wounded shoulder. Quietly, he began recounting events, beginning with his last hours in Manorwood.

Smidge listened intently, analyzing every word and gesture to determine if the beast was telling the truth. He waited impatiently to discover what had happened the night his father entered the woods, never to be seen again.

"I thought if I made enough noise and charged at them in the darkness, the cowards would retreat. I screamed at the top of my lungs and ran toward the leaders. Everything worked perfectly until I chased them around some boulders deep in the woods. Then, a trip-wire took me down. I fought with every bit of strength I had left and a dozen rats died before their leader, Jakbo, an enormous rat, managed to tie me up. They dragged me back to Magnath to be a slave, but when the king heard of my fighting skills, he offered me a deal. He constantly feared for his life and needed his most trusted soldier, Jakbo, close to him. Only a big, strong fighter could control the army, so he offered me a deal. As long as I led his troops, he would never attack Manorwood again. If I did not agree, he'd give orders the next day to burn Manorwood to the ground and kill everyone."

"So that's why, for all these seasons, our village has never been attacked."

"Yes." Uncontrolled shudders shook Terramboe's massive shoulders, and he could barely finish. "I didn't know what to do. They were always spying on me to make sure I did what they wanted. What I've done was not right, Smidge. But I've done it so you and your mother and everyone else I loved would be safe."

Smidge lowered his sword and began unbuckling the heavy black armour from his father's shoulders. He let it fall to the ground. Once the last vestige of Magnath's evil was gone, he wrapped his arms around his weeping father and hugged him hard.

"It's time to come home now, Dad."

"But no one will understand, Smidge."

"I understand, Dad, and so will Mom—that is what's important. Everyone else will only know that you were held captive and that we rescued you. Now, let's get that wound washed and dressed properly and find you some different clothes. We don't want any more mistakes made about who you are."

Crowds of slaves and soldiers making their way out of the fortress slowed their crossing to the Royal Chambers. "Son, have you captured the king?"

"No, he and the captain of the guard deserted the queen."

Terramboe grunted. "Figures. Let's keep going."

Approaching the palace, Terramboe stopped in his tracks and pulled Smidge against the wall of a stone staircase leading up to the ramparts. A glint of gold had caught his eye. Behind piles of debris and broken wooden barrels he caught a glimpse of a red tunic. The Royal Guards! Where they were, there would be Jakbo and the king. Of course! What better way for a couple of cowards to escape than down the garbage chute?

Grabbing a sword from a fallen rat, Terramboe grabbed Smidge's arm. "Let's go. I have unfinished business." Forgetting his arrow wound, he raced behind the palace.

"Dad, where are you going? What about your arm?"

"No worries, I am right-pawed." He waved the sword with his good arm and charged on, with Smidge close behind.

Rounding the corner, they came upon several Royal Guards hoisting one of their own up into the wooden chute through the outer wall. Their once beautiful gold and red tunics were soiled and tattered.

Jakbo turned to face the intruders with a menacing look.

"Well, well, well, look who we have here." The enormous rat unsheathed his sword with a swoosh of grating metal. "The king is long gone, and you, Terramboe, have outlived your usefulness." Teeth bared, he descended upon Terramboe with terrifying ferocity.

Terramboe barely had time to raise his sword before the first blow landed. He struck back with several good swings, but weakened, and with only one arm, the once powerful otter proved no match for his aggressor. Stumbling backward, he fell awkwardly on the remains of a barrel.

Smidge had been warily watching to see if the other rats would attack, but they were only interested in escape. Seeing his father's arm drop, succumbing to the onslaught of the rat's two-pawed blows, he jumped between them. Timing his thrust, he lunged with all his might as the rat raised his sword, exposing his flank.

Jakbo yelped and stood back. Unfazed, he turned his gaze to Smidge and sneered, "Ah, good—two for one."

Swinging his blade across his chest and downward, he smashed Smidge's small sword from his paw, sending it clattering across the stones below. So quick was the movement that Smidge felt a rush of air pass by his face. Startled, he stood watching the big rat raise his sword for the next strike.

"Manorwood!" shouted a chorus of voices behind Smidge. He turned to see Mash, Marta and Pete rushing toward him. Marta slowed and tossed her beautiful, huge sword his way.

Catching and swinging the weapon in one fell swoop, Smidge slashed at the belly of his surprised opponent. Jakbo stumbled back. Smidge charged forward with the sword held high. The others rushed forward and joined him, all of them screaming together, "Attack Brigade! Attack!"

Jakbo turned and fled, disappearing into the garbage chute. By the time the brigade leaders looked to the garbage heap below, there were no rats to be seen.

EPILOGUE

Smidge's friends were ecstatic. Terramboe was alive, contrary to what the queen had told them. Gerr was speechless. He hugged his brother and pounded him so enthusiastically on the back that he nearly knocked the wind out of him. Smidge joined the celebration, and the three of them held their embrace for a long time. Mash, Marta, Alex and Pete exchanged proud looks and high-fived while they witnessed the joyful reunion.

The first thing father and son did together after the bandaging of Terramboe's wound was to visit "Aswar"'s chambers. Wincing from the pain of his wound, the otter crouched beside his former bed and withdrew a small wooden box. After opening the lid with shaking paws, he removed the tattered piece of parchment that was the box's only content.

Smidge smiled as he looked at the crude, yet magnificently detailed, drawing of Manorwood. Along the edge was written every inhabitant's name and relationship. The last two entries were, "Silk and Smidge, my wife, my son."

Terramboe held the parchment gently and his voice broke as he tried to explain. "After every battle, I came here and looked at this picture and thought about you and your mother and all my friends in Manorwood. It helped to ease the pain of what I felt I had to do."

Smidge said nothing. After a moment, he carefully returned the paper to its box and helped his father to his paws. Then, silently, they returned to the others.

❧

A memorial service was held the following day. The surviving Farlanders, Flyers, Woodlanders and Manorwood soldiers buried their dead. Each grave was marked with a plaque of honour. After a few days of rest, the Manorwood Brigade parted company with their comrades in arms. They shook paws and embraced with deep emotion, having shared the experience of facing death and surviving.

Always the adventurer, Trouter decided to go to Manorwood to see where his otter friends lived before journeying home. One Eye gladly accepted Long Flight's invitation to stay with the Flyers while he rested from the recent battle. The long misunderstanding between his tribe and the Flyers had been put to rest forever.

Bolt, who felt too old to start a new life outside of Magnath, was left in charge of the fortress. Many of the other homeless slaves planned to form a peace-loving community there, but were prepared to keep away any rats who chose to retake the stronghold. Thus, the first act of the new rulers of Magnath was to empty the weapons rooms and arm themselves against any future attacks.

Terramboe, wanting to return the kindness shown to him by the queen, encouraged the victors to set her free. Afterwards, Smidge couldn't stop laughing about Pete's suggestion that the queen live with Miss Marple. What a pair of rats they would make!

On the day of their departure, the once ragtag Manorwood Brigade marched proudly with crisp precision out of the main gate. In tight formation, with their heads held high, they raised their swords in a farewell salute to the former slaves. Alex, Pete, Smidge, Gerr and Terramboe strode shoulder-to-shoulder at the head of the formation. Mash, Marta and Grunch followed behind. All three held paws, chattering non-stop about where in the Valley of Stone the young couple would build a house.

Smidge looked over at his dad and smiled broadly. "Mom sure is going to be mad at me."

"I am certain she'll understand, son. I just hope she doesn't mind setting another place at the dinner table."

"She has been, Dad, the whole time you were gone."

Putting his arms around his son as they walked together, Terramboe grinned. "Let's go home, son."

"By the way, Dad, I am a pretty good juggler now. I'll show you when we get home."

Pete groaned so loudly that every creature broke into hearty laughter.

ACKNOWLEDGMENTS

Attack of the Manorwood Brigade began as a Christmas gift for my two young sons. I had spun many rainy-day and bedtime yarns, but wanted to create something that would remind my boys of the hours we spent curled up on the couch, or in the tree fort. What began as a small project grew from a few pages into a book, which the boys eventually received a few Christmases ago. With the encouragement of family and friends, I decide to pursue publishing the manuscript.

The story has been improved by the suggestions of many. Thank you to Jane Willms for your help and encouragement and to the editing crew at Granville Island Publishing: David, Jo, Alisha and Neall. Thanks to Gordon for bringing the images of the characters out of my imagination and onto the pages.

JOHNNY MAY was born in London, Ontario. There, his love of music blossomed into a successful songwriting career that he balances with his love of telling stories, his work as a physician in Guelph and his volunteer service at medical outreach clinics in Guatemala. He recently released an album entitled *Alone In This Together*, which is available on iTunes and at www.johnnymaymusic.ca.

The author's quirky animal characters, inspired by friends and family and influenced by his earlier career as a biologist studying small creatures, were invented to entertain his two young sons. These yarns eventually became the *Magnath Chronicles*.